P9-DCH-588

ERASE AND REWIND

ERASE AND REWIND

Stories

Meghan Bell

Book*hug Press

TORONTO

FIRST EDITION
copyright © 2021 by Meghan Bell
ALL RIGHTS RESERVED

No part of this publication may be reproduced or transmitted in any form
or by any means, electronic or mechanical, including photocopying, recording,
or any information storage or retrieval system, without permission in writing
from the publisher.

Library and Archives Canada Cataloguing in Publication
Title: Erase and rewind : stories / Meghan Bell.
Names: Bell, Meghan, author.
Identifiers: Canadiana (print) 20210162481 | Canadiana (ebook) 20210162678
 ISBN 9781771666787 (softcover)
 ISBN 9781771666794 (EPUB)
 ISBN 9781771666800 (PDF)
Classification: LCC PS8603.E4493 E73 2021 | DDC C813/.6—dc23

The production of this book was made possible through the generous
assistance of the Canada Council for the Arts and the Ontario Arts Council.
Book*hug Press also acknowledges the support of the Government of Canada
through the Canada Book Fund and the Government of Ontario through the
Ontario Book Publishing Tax Credit and the Ontario Book Fund.

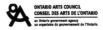

Book*hug Press acknowledges that the land on which we operate is the traditional
territory of many nations, including the Mississaugas of the Credit, the
Anishnabeg, the Chippewa, the Haudenosaunee, and the Wendat peoples. We
recognize the enduring presence of many diverse First Nations, Inuit, and Métis
peoples and are grateful for the opportunity to meet and work on this territory.

CONTENTS

ERASE AND REWIND

DAY TWELVE

Louisa discovered she could reverse time on a dim suburban street, thirty-eight minutes after leaving Nick's house.

It happened by accident: she stepped in dog shit. The shit squished over the soles of her sandals, wrapping around her naked feet and between her toes. She stopped walking and screamed breathlessly into the night.

If it hadn't been so dark, she could have avoided the shit. If she'd been watching, if she'd been paying attention, if she hadn't been staring at the stoplights three blocks ahead, wondering if they seemed so bright because of the marijuana she'd smoked hours before or because of the gelatinous tears stuck on her corneas like contact lenses. If none of those things, she probably would have seen the shit and she probably would have avoided it.

Louisa thought about all of this, when she realized she was walking backwards. She felt her foot step into the imprint she'd left in the shit, toe-heel, and then lift, dry, and step back onto clean concrete. She looked down and her feet stopped moving. She was standing directly behind the shit, which was now—miraculously—intact.

A string of complicated and contradicting emotions exploded in her gut. She had stepped in dog shit, and she had reversed it. How was this possible? Yet, there it was, footprint-free, right in front of her eyes.

Or had it even happened? The memory blurred at the edges. She remembered *remembering* that she had stepped in dog shit, but she couldn't recall the sensation.

No. She had reversed it. She must have. She'd been so sure a minute ago.

Louisa pulled her cellphone out of her purse and checked the time. 12:33 a.m.

She closed her eyes and thought *back*.

Her eyes opened. She couldn't move. She stared at the dog shit for what felt like a long time, and then, automatically, she began to walk backwards. After a block she forced herself to break the trance again. She checked the time. 12:24 a.m. She waited until the four became a five before lifting her chin. Already, she could barely remember the block ahead.

She not only could rewind, Louisa realized. She could erase.

The sadness within her burst and spread like lava. It grew out from her gut down into the dull pain between her legs and up her torso, where it seared her heart, then wound its way through her limbs. The weight of it was unbearable. It threatened to drown all other feelings.

She closed her eyes and thought *back*.

DAY ELEVEN

Louisa had only looked back once after she left Nick's house, at exactly 11:59 p.m. on Saturday night.

When her head began to turn, she felt a sharp sense of relief. In horror movies, the mounting tension before the audience sees the monster is always more terrifying than the monster itself. Louisa watched a lot of horror movies.

It was just an ordinary student house. Faded blue paint chipped and fell on the overgrown lawn. Empty forties of liquor littered windowsills. Automatically, her head tilted away from her shoulder and her gaze returned to the ground. She continued to step back toward her destination. Small tears rolled up her face and into her eyes.

Back, back.

Louisa stepped backwards up the three porch steps. Her hand shot back, and the doorknob swung to meet her palm.

She'd rushed out of the house, and now she rushed back into it, winding her way through the foyer and up the staircase, to his bedroom door, and inside.

Nick sat upright in bed, the fly of his jeans open, his body twisted toward the open window. He was shirtless, and the slight paunch of his stomach peeked over his *Simpsons* boxers. He leaned outside and inhaled clouds of smoke. Each time he lifted the joint to his lips, it burned bright and lengthened like Pinocchio's nose.

They both started speaking. Their voices were guttural, haunting. Louisa imagined conspiracy theorists listening for Satanic messages in their reverse dialect. She couldn't understand a word, and when she tried to remember what had been said the first time they'd lived this scene, she started mentally humming the lyrics to "Baby, It's Cold Outside," which, for whatever reason, she found so perversely hysterical she started to giggle or maybe vomit, and Nick and his bedroom froze for a fraction of a second, then he began to speak.

"Ha, you're so stoned," Nick said. "Seriously, just crash here."

Shit. Louisa focused, and Nick repeated the words in reverse.

She dropped her purse on the desk, shrugged off her cardigan, and kneeled to fiddle with the straps of her sandals. Her hands and vision shook—she was getting drunker and higher with each receding minute. She heard a lighter click and the roll of the spark wheel, and then the sounds of Nick returning the joint to the small Tupperware he kept in his bedside table. She stood and pulled down her underwear, and returned them to where they had been lost in the sheets. She sat on the bed and waited. Then, in a single movement, she hinged down until she lay on the bed with her arms over her head.

Nick hovered above her. One hand clamped over her wrists, the other pinning down her left shoulder. His face was triumphant. As the look faded and he pressed down into her, Louisa unopened her eyes and reminded herself that this soon would be erased.

Close to the beginning, she said something that sounded a bit like *own. Own*, she said. Then again, softer: *own.*

It took her a moment to flip the sounds. A weird sense of vindication washed through her.

She knew she'd told him she didn't want to have sex when she'd agreed to go home with him, back when they were dancing in the bar.

With a nudge at her ribs, he'd bet her he could change her mind.

She laughed. "Oh, like you're *that* good?"

He grinned. Nick had a soft face, and a pair of dimples that made him seem gentle and a little goofy. He'd delivered the warning like a joke, and Louisa had ribbed back, oblivious to the punchline.

Until now, she hadn't been able to remember if she'd said *no* after that.

You fucking asshole, she thought.

Each thrust was more painful than the one before it, until he finally pulled out for good and the wound was healed.

THREE THINGS TO KNOW ABOUT LOUISA:

1. A couple years ago, inspired by celebrities like Beyoncé and Emma Watson, Louisa and the group of girls she befriended in her first year of university began to identify as feminists. That Christmas, they all exchanged copies of *The Feminine Mystique*, *The Beauty Myth*, *Bad Feminist*, and autobiographies by famous comediennes like Tina Fey. Ever the diligent student, Louisa took to the internet to learn as much about the different movements as possible. She quickly realized that not only was she impossibly ignorant, but the more she learned, the more ignorant she felt. She found some of the more extreme—a word she would only use in her head—content difficult to relate to. Consequently, while she identified as a feminist and dedicated hours each week to reading articles, think-pieces, essays, and books by feminist writers, Louisa had never written a single internet comment, tweet, or Facebook post on the subject of feminism and preferred to hold her tongue

in conversations that touched on feminist politics—or politics in general. Not because she was afraid of a right-wing backlash (although she was, a little), but because she was afraid of getting feminism *wrong*—like her idols, Beyoncé, Emma Watson, and Tina Fey all had in some way or the other, according to the internet.

2. Louisa lost her virginity at seventeen to her high school boyfriend. This was something she neither regretted, nor recalled with any sort of particular fondness. She had since slept with two other people, both boyfriends she'd been dating for at least three months. She liked to joke that her relative "prudishness" was a result of "recessive Catholic DNA." (Louisa was a math major, and hadn't studied biology since tenth grade.) No one in Louisa's family believed in God or went to church—other than for weddings and funerals—but seven of her eight great-grandparents had been devout. However, the secret truth was that Louisa was a bit of prude because she was a bit of a romantic, which was just one of the many traits that made her suspect she was absolutely useless at feminism.

3. At this time, there were 423 photographs chronicling Louisa's experimentations with alcohol, marijuana, and—just one time, at a deadmau5 concert—ecstasy, which were available online through her and her friends' various social media profiles. Eleven of those pictures were taken within the last four hours. Nick was in three of them, and in one,

they are standing outside the bar, sharing a joint, both smiling drunk like they didn't have a care in the world.

DAY TEN

Falling out of sleep was like floating to the surface of a deep lake.

As Louisa slowly regained consciousness, a complication occurred to her: if she allowed time to start moving forward and didn't remember Nick was a threat, how was she supposed to make sure he didn't do it again?

She could write herself a note before her memory started to fade, but would she believe it? And even if she did, they still spent three hours per week in a classroom together, and they were technically "seeing each other," even if it had only been eight days. She'd have to drop the class. She'd have to text him that they were breaking up. This struck sober Louisa as both wildly inconvenient and potentially dangerous. So she kept rewinding.

Louisa had always prided herself on being a rational, pragmatic person. Like many people, she had little to no control over her emotions when she drank, but now she folded them up and tucked them into the analytical creases of her left brain. She wondered, as she turned and tossed to the faint backwards soundtrack of her roommate watching *Grey's Anatomy*, if it would have been better to not rewind, and just deal with the events of that night. She pushed the thought out of her mind. The fact was, the idea of going to the police or telling anyone what happened terrified her. It was better to relive this terrible thing if it meant she wouldn't have to deal with the emotional and physical consequences. The decision to rewind had been made through the lens of tequila, marijuana, and a high level of distress, but Louisa suspected she would have made the exact same call dead sober.

Louisa was not the sort of person who believed that *everything happens for a reason*. The human brain is designed to identify patterns and order, and where little to none exists, impose it. Louisa found the concept of destiny and the people who believed in it to be terribly boring and depressing.

The rational thing to do, Louisa decided, would be to erase the whole fucking relationship.

THREE PROBLEMS WITH LOUISA'S STORY (THREE REASONS NOT TO GO TO THE POLICE):

1. When Nick pulled down her underwear, she laughed and said, "Hey! Don't do that!" but did not physically try to stop him. She knew this because he said, "You're not stopping me." She then continued to not stop him because his pants were on anyway, and the situation was awkward, and for reasons she would never understand, Louisa did not interpret the removal of her underwear as threatening. She was still trying to figure out how to politely tell him she wanted her underwear back when it became too late. This could be interpreted as consent.

2. She did not realize that Nick had unzipped his own fly until he was already inside of her. He entered her without

warning and so quickly it hurt like hell, and Louisa gasped in pain. She was still thinking about how much it fucking hurt when Nick asked her, already thrusting, whether or not she was on the pill. She answered reflexively: "Yeah." This could be interpreted as consent.

3. Although Louisa did say "no" a total of three times and tried to push Nick off her, there was a chance, she supposed, that he had neither heard nor felt her try to fight him off on account of the fact that Louisa was very drunk, very stoned, and had roughly the upper-arm strength of a hamster. She stopped fighting after a few minutes and let it happen. After about fifteen minutes, desperate for the whole fucking thing to *just be over*, she pretended to moan and lifted her neck to gently bite his ear, which was something that had made her last boyfriend come immediately. It had ended a minute later, and recalling that, Louisa could not figure out if the intense feeling of relief she'd had when he pulled out equalled the intense feelings of guilt and shame she had about the goddamn ear-nibble, like she had betrayed herself, betrayed feminism, and betrayed society by becoming just another data point supporting the fucking theory that a woman's *no* is just a *yes* that needs a little encouragement. This could be interpreted as consent.

DAY NINE

The secret to reversing time, Louisa quickly realized, was to separate mind and body. She pictured her "mental" self as a tiny homunculus, spinning on its haunches in the back of her brain while her "physical" self, her body, followed the choreography being unwritten from her life thread. As long as her mental self didn't order her physical self to do anything once the rewind was going, time would continue to passively march backwards. For the most part, Louisa tried not to think about what her physical self was doing at all.

On Thursday, she started creating elaborate fantasies to pass the hours. Many of them involved horrible and/or violent things happening to Nick. When she got bored or creeped out by the fantasies, she tried to solve complicated probability questions in her head.

Louisa calculated the fraction of hours she had rewound and how much further she had to go. She and Nick had met on the second day of the September semester in a 12:30 p.m. astronomy seminar they were both taking as an easy elective. This meant they had known each other for 252 hours when Louisa began to rewind time. As her body brushed tangles into her hair on Thursday night and typed away inane chat messages to Nick, her mind followed her eyes when they darted up to the clock in the top-right corner of her laptop, and after a couple of quick calculations realized, with a slight thrill, that she was already a fifth of the way there.

DAY EIGHT

Nick and Louisa had spent most of Wednesday afternoon in a local coffee bar, picking away at their respective formulas. The sunset backlit Nick. The electric candle on the table between them cast light up on his face at a sharp angle that splintered when it hit his thick-framed glasses, leaving two long shadows over his eyebrows that reminded Louisa of a cartoon villain.

She caught a glimpse of the time on the face of her cell-phone when her hand lifted it from the table and turned it toward Nick. 7:47 p.m.

Seventy-six hours and forty-three minutes down, she thought, as her body smiled and warmed in response to a kiss Nick was about to remove from her nose. Three-tenths of the way there.

It was here, at the one hundred and seventy-fifth hour of their relationship, that Louisa first considered whether her crush on Nick could grow into something more. She found him charming, smart, and cute, but there was something off-putting, like she felt an overwhelming need to impress him and because of that she couldn't quite get comfortable, and she wasn't sure whether that was because she liked him so much or because she didn't like him nearly as much as she thought she did. She remembered the conversation leading up to this thought so perfectly she could hear the words even as they were spoken in reverse.

Nick: You're adorable.

Louisa (laughing): I don't know! I thought it was funny that I thought it!

Nick: Why'd you say it then?

Louisa: That didn't even sound clever in my head.

Nick (laughing): You should be.

Louisa (laughing): I'm sorry.

Nick: Nope, shut it down. That's the worst.

Louisa (air-quoting): Like, "Nick"-name.

Nick (silence):
Louisa: Nickname!
Nick: What?
Louisa (laughing):
Nick: I think it's cute. Could be a nickname for me.
Louisa: Oh no, that's terrible. Shybrows.
Nick: My sha-brows? Shybrows?
Louisa: With your evil shadow-brows.
Nick (taking the phone): I look downright sinister.
Louisa (laughing): Oh my god.
Nick (sinister voice): Beware…my evil plan. Something.
Louisa: Look! This is why I was laughing. Your eyebrows. You look like a freaking cartoon villain.

She pulled back the phone and framed Nick in the screen. At 7:39 p.m., her finger tapped the circle at the bottom and erased the picture forever. *Seventy-six hours and fifty-one minutes down. One hundred and seventy-five hours and nine minutes to go.*

LOUISA'S THREE THEORIES OF TIME REVERSAL:

1. Erased time took several minutes to eclipse and disappear completely after a rewind was stopped and time began to move forward again. Louisa was uncertain whether the rewound memories atrophied at a steady rate or exponentially—in which case, perhaps the faintest outline of the memories could linger.

2. Regardless of whether it was steady or exponential, decay time was most likely affected by both the amount of focus

Louisa put into trying to retain the memories, and by the number and degree of distractions available when she stopped rewinding.

3. Louisa had always been able to reverse time, but she kept forgetting about her power because of Theory #1. She suspected this because she had a hard time recalling anything she'd done that she'd consider to be "big" mistakes. Perhaps she was not such a rational, pragmatic person after all. Perhaps she was just a regular, illogical person blessed with the power to rewind and redo every fuck-up. Maybe tons of terrible things had happened to her—car crashes, bad grades, fights with friends, injuries, sexual assaults, and other troubles—and she'd just erased them all.

DAY SEVEN

Louisa took pleasure in imagining a pie chart slowly disappear, one degree at a time.

It took 104 hours of rewinding before it occurred to her that she might not actually forget anything that had happened to her. She had been pretty confident her memory would be erased, but now while she remembered *remembering* something about dog shit, she wasn't entirely sure what it had to do with time reversal. And the more she thought about *why* she was rewinding, the more she wondered whether any memory loss could have been the result of all the booze and weed she'd consumed. In which case, all three of her theories were likely wrong.

Louisa had no idea what the psychological effects of remembering everything would be, and she didn't want to find out. She was doing this because she believed she would forget everything, and the doubts caused her a great deal of anxiety, so she dismissed them as irrational and dangerous and she suppressed them. For the first time, Louisa thought she understood faith.

DAY SIX

With one hour until the start of astronomy class, Louisa calculated she had reached the halfway point: only 121 hours left to rewind.

Under their desks, her knee tilted against Nick's. She pulled a note out of her purse and unfolded it to reveal a Mickey Mouse-esque doodle of a molecule, with the words *Hey Copper-Titanium, I have my ion you* written in a speech bubble above his head.

Below the speech bubble, in her writing, a question mark.

Below that, in Nick's writing, *CuTi, also a reference to your hair.*

His hand slipped under hers and he pulled the note back to his desk. She watched as, letter by letter, the last sentence disappeared under the nib of his pen, and to her surprise and frustration, she felt more than just a little sad.

DAY FIVE

Louisa fell out of sleep to the glow of her laptop. Her eyes fluttered for twenty or so minutes after they opened fully and she recalled, with annoyance, that she'd fallen asleep while creeping Nick's Facebook page and had left her laptop open to a picture from the summer of 2007—Nick playing road hockey with friends. They would have been about twelve, but Louisa thought they looked a little younger in the photo. She rolled onto her stomach, and her hands fell on the keyboard and touchpad. She started to scroll through his pictures, back to 2016. She clicked the chat tab just as Nick's final *night!* vanished.

As they deleted their conversation line by line, dread slowly built in Louisa like a hunger pang.

Louisa: Breakups are the worst.

Nick: Haha, yeah. I lived there before she moved in though.

Louisa: At least you got custody of the house.

Nick: Yeah, totally.

Louisa: Still sucks though.

Nick: It doesn't matter. No one believed her anyway, and later she admitted she was lying because she was pissed about the breakup.

Louisa: :-(

Nick: Just stupid stuff. Stuff that wasn't true.

Louisa: What did she say??

Nick: Yeeeeeah.

Louisa: Oh, man.

Nick: It's cool. She actually lived here with me and everyone, but we were fighting a lot and kept breaking up and getting back together. When we broke up the last time and she moved out, she shit-talked me and was basically like I hate you so it was kind of brutal.

Louisa: (Sorry if that was super inappropriate, you don't have to answer)

Louisa: What happened?

Nick: No :-(

Louisa: Oh yeah? Civil?

Nick: Civility is good. Haha. Yeah, I just broke up with someone too.

Louisa: Don't be. I broke up with him. It was pretty civil, actually.

Nick: Oh, that sucks. I'm sorry.

Louisa: Well, I actually just broke up with someone and we were together two years and friends before that, so no.

Nick: Date-dates? "Date" dates.

Nick: Do you not go on date dates often?

Louisa: Never mind.

Nick: Haha, what?

THREE THINGS LOUISA REALIZED AS SHE WATCHED THE CONVERSATION DISAPPEAR:

1. She was pretty sure she knew what Nick's ex-girlfriend had said about him.

2. Nick honestly did not think he had done anything wrong to his ex-girlfriend, which meant he honestly had not thought he had done anything wrong to Louisa, which meant:

3. He would do it again.

DAY FOUR

Louisa wanted to disappear. She wanted to fold herself in half, fold herself in half again, then again and again and again and again and again and again until she disappeared completely, which wasn't mathematically possible, but she didn't give a shit. The homunculus in the back of her skull could no longer ignore her body. The homunculus felt seasick from walking backwards all the time. The homunculus was having a nervous breakdown.

Louisa couldn't understand a word she or Nick said as they wound backwards along the seawall, but she hated the way she never took her eyes off him. It was sunny out, but his pupils were dilated, and she suspected hers were as well. Their eyes couldn't get enough of each other. Many of Louisa's revenge fantasies involved Nick confessing his love so she could break his heart, and now, in the back of her own mind as she observed their second date unwind, she wondered whether that meant she still believed he cared for her or, worse, she still secretly wanted him to. It was an illness. She was sick. Her physical self was a mess of clichés, of butterflies in the stomach, heartbeats in her neck and wrists, a natural bending toward him as though opposite poles of a magnet braided through their spines. This stupid, unobservant body that failed to protect her, and the stupid, selfish person inside who would unravel 252 hours just to protect herself, and only herself, from the inconvenience of trauma, victim-blaming, the morning-after pill, and an STI test. Louisa had read about what happened to girls who asked for justice. She didn't want to be one of those girls.

On camping trips her family had taken when she was a child, her father liked to joke about bears. *You don't have to be fast to run from a bear,* he'd say. *You just gotta be faster than the guy next to you.* Nick was the common denominator. If she removed herself from the equation, it didn't mean Nick would no longer be able to date or date-rape. It just meant that he would happen to somebody else, like he had already happened to somebody else. What sort of activist—what sort of feminist—was she, if she was fighting only for herself? Perhaps, Louisa thought, activism is inherently selfish—born from the desire for things to be better for you and people like you. But she immediately realized this was overly simplistic, this was wrong. And anyway, she had never been an activist because she had never been *active.* She was a consumer of activism, she was risk-averse to the point of inertia, too scared to do much more than occasionally hit the "Like" button on Facebook. The sort of person who liked to think she was against *bad things*—like racism and rape culture and homophobia and all the other isms and phobias—but deep down she only meant she was against bad things happening to *her.*

And now there was nothing Louisa could do. There was no going to the police, there was no reaching out to the ex-girlfriend to help her and support her, there was no telling the world what he did. The thing never happened.

In seventy-four hours they wouldn't even know each other.

DAY THREE

Friday. The first date. Nick had suggested a nicer restaurant— in the twenty- to thirty-dollar range. Louisa was surprised when she woke up that night to discover she was tipsy and had been pretty tipsy for most of their date.

She descended the staircase to the foyer of her building, all the way back to their first kiss. She was flooded with warmth when they started, and as they rewound the kiss back to its inception, she grew colder and colder. He released her at the beginning of the kiss almost as quickly as she'd fallen into his arms at the end.

DAY TWO

Louisa nodded and smiled and agreed to the date, and then Nick asked her for it. As he retreated through the crowd of the student union building, Louisa caught a glimpse of a clock above the Starbucks. 2:48 p.m. *Twenty-six hours and eighteen minutes left.* Approximately nine-tenths down, one-tenth to go.

The guilt was iron in her lungs but the rewind was done, she reminded herself, again and again. She wasn't about to relive the relationship so he could assault her again, for a *third* fucking time, just so she could report it. Besides, she didn't realize there were other girls, she didn't know, she'd missed the signs. She was allowed to protect herself. The rewind was done—she couldn't undo it. She had to make the best of the decision. And she couldn't wait to forget she'd ever made it.

DAY ONE

Ninety minutes to go.

Only one…one hundred and sixty-eighth…left. The pie chart was a sliver.

Before Louisa and Nick exchanged contact information, they agreed to trade class notes so as to minimize the amount of work each person was doing for their shared "blow-off" class. Before this, they exchanged names and majors. *Nick, chemistry-slash-pre-med. Louisa, math with a minor in statistics.* They shook hands. Then it was the end of class and the adjunct began to speak.

Louisa counted the number of times she turned her head to admire Nick's profile during this first astronomy class. Forty-six times.

Five minutes left.

Four.

Three.

Two.

She gathered her things and stood. Her body flung itself backwards up the aisle and through the doors. She'd been late because her bus was late and she had sat next to Nick because it was a free aisle seat near the back. *It's funny,* Louisa thought, *how random it was.* She still didn't believe in fate.

Outside the classroom, Louisa ordered her body to stop.

Time froze. Then the people in the hallway were walking forward instead of backwards. Louisa focused. *You are dropping astronomy. You are dropping astronomy. Nick is dangerous and you are dropping astronomy.* Already the memories of the past twelve days were dimming, like they were a dream and she'd just opened her eyes. She pulled a pen out of her bag and wrote on her hand, *drop astronomy.*

A dark-haired girl brushed past her and held open the door. "You going in?"

"Excuse me?"

"This is astronomy, right? You going in?"

Louisa's head felt thick and heavy and muted. Like she had a terrible cold and couldn't form a straight thought. "No," she said. "I'm not. I heard this class is terrible."

"Oh shit, really? I heard it was an easy A."

Louisa felt nauseated. She needed to lie down. She needed to drop this class and sign up for another.

She had to help.

"Don't sit at the back."

"What?"

"Don't sit at the back. Um. I heard the prof has a quiet voice, you won't be able to hear him."

"Oh," the girl said. "Okay."

Louisa nodded. Her eyes fell on her hand: *drop astronomy*.

The girl slid inside the classroom and let the door swing shut behind her.

Louisa turned and walked away.

FAKING IT

The day before our plane caught fire, Karen Phillips brought up lesbians in the change room after our sixth and final game of nationals.

"The Fresh Alberta Beef only beat us," she said, using the nickname we'd assigned to Team Alberta, "because they have a ton of lesbians."

We stared at her uncomfortably. Our coach was openly gay, but Lisa had already left the change room, after announcing that she couldn't stand the stench of our failure, or our body odour. Finally, Jill, our team captain, spoke: "*So?*"

"So lesbians are better athletes. Because they have more testosterone. Like men." Karen said this confidently, which was bizarre coming from a girl who had bragged about how she was barely passing ninth-grade science a few hours earlier at breakfast. When she said stupid shit, which was a lot, some of the other girls joked she'd taken one too many pucks to the head. *A save's a save*, Karen once responded. She was our starting goalie, and the only reason we'd made it to the finals. We'd lost two-nothing, but Alberta outshot us eight to one.

"How the fuck do you know if they're lesbians or not?" Jill asked.

"I was talking to this girl from Manitoba, and she said she saw two of the Alberta girls kissing."

"Where?"

Karen shrugged.

"Okay, fine, but that just proves two of them are lesbians, not the whole team."

"Yeah, that's not a big deal." We all looked at Juliet. She lay supine on the bench, shirtless, her left leg stretched perpendicular in the air with her arms locked around it. Her track pants had fallen to the knee, revealing a large black bruise on her calf. "I mean, like five per cent of people are gay, or something like that." She sat up and pulled her hoodie on over her sports bra. Our outfits matched both on and off the ice. Off the ice, we wore black track pants and apple-green hoodies. Juliet was one of the few girls on the team who could wear the colour without looking ill. "Seventeen girls...chances are one of us is a lesbian." She grinned and then, to my horror, met my gaze. "Wonder who it is?" Her hoodie was still open.

I tried not to react, not to blush, not to look away too quickly.

"Lisa. Duh. She counts, one out of eighteen. Close to five per cent," Jill said. She zipped up her bag and picked it up, ready to go. "Fuck, Karen, don't be such a homophobe." She smacked her hand against the side of her head, the team signal for brain damage.

Due to a shortage of chaperones, almost everyone was sharing a bed with a teammate for the week. It was obvious Juliet felt that she drew the short straw when she got stuck with me. She was tolerant enough of me when we were alone, but the second we were with the team, she'd bolt, like being a loser who was aggressively mediocre at hockey was contagious or something. I was unpopular both off and on the ice. In every team picture, I'm always standing near the edge of the frame. Sometimes I'm missing an arm or a leg, sometimes I'm bisected; one eye, half a torso, half a nose, half a smile, and half an apple-green team hoodie.

On our final night in Calgary, the senior girls had plans to "rookie" the new ones. The name was a misnomer since the team threw the dinner at the end of the season instead of the start. It was more of a send-off to the senior girls, a night where we were allowed to dress up like idiots and eat greasy food after months of cutting it from our diets. Most of the team had spent the whole tournament looking forward to it. Even though I was almost fifteen and would move on to Midget hockey with all the senior girls in September, I hadn't made the team last year so I was still technically a rookie.

Juliet grabbed a bulging black garbage bag from her suitcase and told me we were going over to Jill's room. Three other rookies were already there: Sam, who was the second-highest scorer on our team; Natsuko, who before this year had always played with boys; and Marion, who was the same age as me but one of the last girls cut from last year's team. Both beds were covered with makeup, Halloween costumes, old hockey gear, neon spandex, feather boas, tubes of glitter, and clunky costume jewellery.

Jill teased Suko's hair for almost twenty minutes, until she resembled Helena Bonham Carter in *Sweeney Todd*. Marion was fitted with vampire fangs and a musty pair of children's shoulder pads Juliet had brought along in her bag. They actually *fought* over who would do Sam's makeup, until Jill pushed Juliet out of the way. "Captain's pick!" she said. "You do Annie's."

Juliet turned to me, her face blank with boredom. She layered purple eyeshadow on my lids up to my eyebrows, in a perfunctory way, like she was washing dishes or taking out the garbage, not even bothering to switch the colour for each eye. She handed me a neon-orange tank top to pull over my shirt, and a pair of Chicks With Sticks boxer shorts, with the tags still attached, to pull over my jeans. A spasm of envy rippled through me; Juliet had physically yanked off Marion's sweater, pulled the shoulder pads over her head, and fastened the Velcro bands over her chest and around her arms. Once I was dressed, she pulled my dark hair back into two lopsided pigtails that were careless more than deliberate.

I glanced over her shoulder at the mirror that hung over the two queen beds. The other girls were mashed up in a way that could only be a costume or a game. I looked like an awkward kid from an eighties movie. Not weird enough for people to be entirely sure this wasn't just how I chose to dress myself. I'd considered the possibility that I'd get the ugliest outfit and the messiest makeup because I was unpopular, but Juliet's indifference was unexpected. I looked down at my thighs; the little yellow chickens on the boxers blurred together, so their hockey sticks appeared to hook into each other's necks.

I would have done anything to wear Juliet's old, sweaty shoulder pads.

As if she'd read my mind, Juliet reached into the bag she'd brought with her and pulled out a single elbow pad. She grabbed my left arm and strapped it around my elbow, over my shirt.

"Might be tight," she said. "It's mine from when I was like ten."

I smiled at her gratefully, but she'd already moved on to douse Suko with a tin of glitter.

For the rest of the night—on the bus, in the restaurant, on the table as I sang Queen's "We Are the Champions" with the rest of the rookies, changing the words in the chorus: "champions" for "losers," "fighting" for "losing," "losers" for "winners"—my elbow tingled with her phantom fingertips.

The next day, we took off on a late-afternoon flight.

Several girls looked exhausted, hungover. Juliet hadn't come back to our room until after two in the morning. My mom, who was sitting a few rows back from me with the rest of the parent chaperones, had spent the night asking me why I didn't try harder to fit in with the team, why I didn't practise more, and then berated Juliet over breakfast for bailing on us, for not inviting me along, even though I'd begged her not to say anything.

You worried us, she'd said. *What am I supposed to tell your parents?*

Juliet had rolled her eyes, which were raccooned with mascara. I noticed she wasn't wearing a bra under her team hoodie. She noticed that I noticed, and later, as Lisa drove the rental bus to the airport, I saw her whisper something to two of the wingers, and then all three of them looked right at me.

Fuck you, I wanted to mouth. Instead I averted my eyes, like I had been looking out the window behind them the whole time.

On the plane, I sat with Lisa and our other goalie, Rachel, the only player who had spent more time on the bench this week than I had. I had the window seat; Lisa, who was six foot one, had the aisle. Between us, Rachel kneeled to talk to Jill, Sam, and Juliet, who were behind us. A flight attendant asked her to sit down when the seat-belt light went on. I stared out the window, but my view was blocked by the wing of the plane. Once we were in the air, I turned my iPod on and shoved my earbuds in, tuned out to sad men singing sad songs: the National, Wilco, the Smiths, Elliott Smith, and the Shins.

Last night, the rookies finished singing and jumped down from the table as the server arrived to take our order. When he left, Juliet and a few others got up to go to the bathroom. Conversation buzzed around me, but I couldn't find one to latch on to, so I tore, twisted, and tied my napkin into a paper doll. I wasn't good at group events. I didn't know how to insert myself into conversations... It seemed like someone else was always talking. Sometimes I tried to laugh when other people laughed, smile when they smiled, nod when they agreed, but a strange distance remained, like we were observing each other through a window. And the more I pretended to connect, the more I was convinced everyone could see I was faking it.

I finished my doll in minutes and balanced her on her skirt, next to a pitcher of soda. At the end of the night, I brought her back to the hotel with me and put her in my suitcase. At home, I had a collection of napkin dolls from different restaurants. I had folded her skirt so the restaurant's logo faced out along her hem.

I decided to go to the bathroom.

Five girls huddled in a circle near the hand towels. When I opened the door, Suko quickly put her hands behind her back, but I could still see the flask in the mirror.

"Hey," I said.

"Hey," Juliet said.

"You guys drinking?"

"No," Karen said. Then she giggled.

"I can see the flask," I said. "In the mirror."

Karen stepped behind Suko, blocking it from my view.

"Well, it's too late *now*," Sam said to Karen. She looked at me. "You going to tell Lisa?"

"No," I said.

Juliet punched Sam in the shoulder. "Of course she's not going to tell, right, Annie?"

"Yeah," I said. "I wouldn't do that."

"See?"

The door opened behind me. "You guys gotta get back out there, Lisa's getting suspicious." Jill didn't look surprised, just sort of bored.

Juliet nodded, and offered Jill the flask.

She shook her head.

"Dude," Juliet said. "You were way more fun last year."

"Last year I wasn't captain," Jill said.

Juliet waved her hand at Jill's face as she brushed past her and out the door, tucking the flask back into her purse. The other four girls followed.

"Fucking stupid," Jill said. "The fuck's the point of getting drunk? There's nothing to do here anyway." She looked at me. "Hey. You okay?"

I wasn't. "Yeah, I'm fine."

Jill nodded. "Juliet's full of shit," she said suddenly. "She claims everyone is in love with her. She just likes the idea of the drama."

I felt hollow. "Is she saying I'm in love with her?"

"Whatever. You won't have to fucking deal with her next year."

This was true. Juliet was certain to make the Midget AA team next year, if she didn't make the Lower Mainland's AAA team. I didn't have a chance in hell at either.

Jill misread the look on my face. "Hey, you know, if you do like her, no judgment."

"Even if I were gay," I spat, "I like to think I'd have better taste than that."

"Totally."

I went into a stall. When I came out, Jill was gone.

You're angry. You're not hurt. I opened my eyes. Through the window, sparks flickered out of the turbine and over the wing of the plane.

I blinked. Was that normal?

More sparks, then flames.

Either no one else had noticed, or it was normal.

If I pointed it out, and there was something wrong, what could we even do? We were two thousand feet above the Rocky Mountains. It's not like the pilot could crawl out on the wing to fix it.

If I pointed it out, and it was normal, I'd look like an idiot. Either we were going to die or we weren't.

Why worry about it.

Right?

I watched as a handful of flames blinked out into the night.

Then: turbulence flung me forward in my seat. I scrambled to fasten my belt. The lights in the plane went out. The lights came back on, then flickered. The plane rocked, like a child had snatched us from the sky and was shaking us in his fist. I still had my earbuds in: it took me almost a second to realize, over the sound of Wilco's "I Am Trying to Break Your Heart," that people around me had started to scream.

It was a Monday night, so the flight was not sold-out. I guessed the plane was about two-thirds full, with eighty or so people, including the attendants and pilots. Of these eighty or so people, twenty-eight were with North Shore Bantam Girls AA hockey team. I imagined our team picture on the cover of newspapers. They would talk about Jill's natural leadership, how Karen was destined for the Olympics, the tragedy of Suko's six-year-old brother, Kaz, who had come along for the trip with her and her mother. Photographs of Kaz with his face pressed against the Plexiglas during one of our games, Suko's oversized team hoodie trailing at his ankles, would be stolen from Facebook and published

again and again and again. I would stand forever at the edge
of the pictures, and the story.

I pulled my earbuds out.

Next to me, Rachel white-knuckled her armrests. She saw
me look at her. "How are you calm?"

I thought about it. "I don't know," I said. "I figure if we're
going to die, freaking out about it is just wasting the time we
have left."

It was the wrong thing to say. Rachel burst into tears.

"What's your problem?" Lisa reached over to comfort her,
and Rachel turned to bury her face in the thick muscle of
Lisa's bare shoulder. I heard her whisper either *fuck you* or
thank you.

Everywhere I looked, people either were panicking or
comforting people who were panicking. Only a handful of us
didn't do anything. I wondered if maybe the people who
didn't react were the sort of people who wanted to comfort
someone, but didn't have anyone to comfort. Or maybe they
didn't know how to react.

I heard a wail behind me. I twisted my body to look over
the seat. Juliet's delicate face was swollen and red, snot and
tears and saliva dripping from her orifices. She had her tray
down and was frantically writing on a piece of lined paper.
Jill and Sam had their hands on her arm and her shoulder.
"You're okay, Jules," Jill said. "Everything will be okay."

"Is she all right?" I asked.

Sam shook her head.

"What's she writing?"

"A goodbye note," Sam said.

Juliet snorted back a sob.

It was the stupidest fucking thing I'd ever heard. If the plane crashed and we all died, there was little to no chance that a small scrap of loose-leaf paper would survive and be read. Juliet was pouring her stupid guts out to create yet another part of her to be destroyed. I opened my mouth to say all this, but closed it when Jill looked up at me. She was repeating, "Everything will be okay, everything will be okay," but her confidence didn't reach her eyes.

Over the intercom, the captain explained that a bird must have flown into the right turbine. He begged us not to panic. "Folks, we're going to turn around and fly back on the other engine. Please remain seated with your seat belts firmly fastened and your seats and trays in the upright position as we begin our descent back to Calgary." The cabin lights went out and this time they didn't come back on.

I looked for my mom over the rows, but all I could see was a slice of her auburn hair. I wondered if she was afraid. I turned to sit back down in my seat.

"Jules, give me the paper," Jill said. "I need to put your tray up. Did you hear what the captain said? We're about to land."

Out the window, sparks were swallowed by the night as soon as they were born. It was sort of beautiful, really, like the turbine was filled with sparklers, or candles on a birthday cake.

I began to sob.

"Annie? Are you okay?" Lisa reached over Rachel for me. "What's going on?"

"Annie, don't cry, we're all good, you heard the captain."

Rachel turned to me. My tears mirrored hers. She hugged me. "Is everything okay?"

"Yeah. Jill, don't worry. Keep talking to Juliet."

"Annie, are you okay?"

"No!" I practically shouted, and buried my face on Rachel's shoulder. She tightened her grip on me. Lisa stretched her arm to hold us both. I collapsed, like the strings lifting me up had been snipped. I closed my eyes as the plane began its descent. I thought about the bird that had been sucked into the engine and wondered why it chose to fly so high and alone.

MOST LIKELY
TO BREAK

The day before my first day of high school, my older sister, Sara, gave me some advice I still follow today.

"Be nice to weird people," she said. "You never know who will end up being a school shooter."

I don't know whether she meant this literally or not, but I understood her meaning to be: *Don't be the sort of person who provokes vengeance in others.* I wasn't sure whether she was referring to herself as the provocateur or the provoked. Sara was sixteen at the time, in the final tailspin of an angst-ridden punk-rock phase that culminated five months later when she was suspended for digging her nails into the arm of a twelfth-grade boy at a school dance, drawing blood. When I asked her why she'd done it, she said he'd assaulted her, but when I told her to go to the school or to the police, she recanted and clarified: "It was the sort of thing that wasn't consensual, but also wasn't bad enough to be entirely non-consensual." I said I was confused and she told me I would understand when I was older. And true to her word, one day I was older, and I understood.

By the time she was twenty-five, Sara had gotten rid of her dark clothes and let her natural honey-brown hair grow out to replace the black she'd dyed twice a month throughout her teen years. She got her degree in physiotherapy and moved into a two-bedroom apartment in Kitsilano with her boyfriend, a preppy law student named Dave who talked a lot about politics, the environment, and human rights, and seemed to think this verbal demonstration of self-awareness was enough to cancel out his family wealth and WASPy whiteness. My parents loved him, but I was indifferent. He was the sort of good person who believed he was better than he was, and while his high expectations of Sara struck me as a kind of hypocrisy, I had to admit he brought out a version of her that some might call her best.

I was in the final year of an English degree, paying my way with contract work for a small company that cleaned out foreclosed homes. I wasn't as efficient at hauling out furniture as the guys, but they kept me on because I was willing to tackle the spots that made them cringe, like the kitchen and the bathrooms. The men I worked with could transition from flirtatious to aggressive, chivalrous to condescending, respectful to exclusionary as easily as a professional dancer can shift his weight from foot to foot. They overpronounced my name—*Nah-tah-lee-ah!*—every time they used it. I kept the job for the stories, and I turned the stories into poems, which I sent to literary magazines, which turned the poems into rejection letters. I played it all up as an act of feminism, but after months of this, Sara called me out on the internalized misogyny behind the visage. "There's a part of you that believes you're a better sort of woman because you can play one of the guys," she said. Across the table, Dave snorted with suppressed laughter.

"You're one to talk," I said.

"How so?" Sara said.

"All the co-ed sports."

"For fuck's sake, Natalia, we're talking about your attitude. I don't parade around pretending I'm some sort of pioneer just because I can catch a ball thrown by a man." After she moved out of our parents' conservative stronghold, Sara had learned to channel her natural tendencies toward violence and self-harm into beer-league sports. I once came out to watch one of her and Dave's flag football games and wasn't at all surprised to see her elbow flying into the jaws and guts of her opponents when the ref wasn't looking.

Sara's comment upset me. It wasn't until much later that night that I realized why: I still looked up to her the same way I had when I was thirteen and she was sixteen. To me, Sara embodied a sort of I-don't-give-a-fuck authenticity that I could only mimic, which was in itself a humiliating failure.

For years now I'd kept a careful eye on those who I perceived to be volatile: the drunk, the drugged, and the entitled, the hyper-masculine and those who adopted the narrative of victimhood to justify their behaviour. I practised a sort of intellectualized kindness that curdled in my mouth. *You never know*. I looked for cracks in people; I always picked at least one person in every room who I labelled Most Likely to Break.

At work, that person was the owner's son, Jeremy. Jeremy was a small, immature man trapped in an oversized, intimidating body. I wanted to be a storyteller, and so I often tried to think about how our personalities are shaped by how we move within the world and how the world reacts to us. For example, would Sara have become so conventional if she had not, by sheer coincidence, been born into a body that was conventionally attractive? Even she admitted that her confidence most likely stemmed from a history of acceptance.

Jeremy was prime for this sort of theorizing. He was the sort of person who frequently tripped over both his feet and his tongue, and while he might have been dismissed as irritating in a smaller body, his height (six-five) and thickness (over two hundred pounds) meant he frightened people, and the frustration and resentment this caused him created a feedback loop that gave people—in my opinion—a good reason to be frightened. In a lot of ways, he was a cliché: bemoaning how women always fell for the "bad boys" and ignored "nice guys" like him, and even though I knew this wasn't his fault, the deepness of his voice and the way his neck muscles flexed always made this sound like a threat. The other two men in our team of four hated him and made no secret of it, but I was pathologically friendly. When one, a lean philosophy major named Noah, asked me why, I told him about Sara's advice and he laughed so loud he rattled the closet doors in the bedroom we were gutting and called over our third co-worker, Peter, to share what I had said. It was the first time I recognized my behaviour as a kind of bullying in and of itself. I wanted to take back my words, but the damage had been done.

I excused myself, passing Jeremy in the hall as I exited. I felt his eyes stick to me like a drop of sweat rolling down my spine as I descended the staircase toward the kitchen. I wasn't sure whether he had heard or not but decided to play innocent. We were out in the Fraser Valley on a relatively easy job. Over half the houses we cleaned had once contained a grow-op or a meth lab, but this one seemed to have suffered nothing worse than wine stains, children, and animals. The former owners had taken as many items of value as they could with them. There were long, thick scratches in the laminate floor from the laundry room through the foyer, where they had dragged the washer and dryer outside.

The kitchen was bare on the surface, but when I started opening cupboards I found moulding loaves of bread, musty cereal boxes filled with crumbs, an empty bag of flour, and other waste. The trash bin under the sink was full and so rancid I gagged and nearly bit my tongue.

I grabbed a box of black plastic bags from the front entrance and began emptying the kitchen, dragging each full, stinking bag of garbage out to the curb as I filled it. Upstairs, Noah and Peter pulled a yellowed mattress out to the balcony and tipped it over the side so it fell and landed with a squelching sound on the muddy grass below.

I went back to the kitchen and filled half a bag with the rotting contents of the fridge. Then I opened the freezer door and I couldn't stop myself—I screamed.

Inside was a large orange tabby cat. It was curled up as though it was sleeping, and its face had the relaxed look of a natural death. Its fur, however, splayed out in all directions, like it had been shocked. The freezer had iced over around the creature, locking it firmly in place by its hair. It still had its collar on. I could see that his name had been Rupert.

"Holy fuck, holy fuck, holy fuck," I repeated. I started to shake with laughter and revulsion. "Holy shit *motherfucker*!"

I heard someone rush down the stairs behind me. I turned, worried it would be Jeremy, and was relieved to see Noah instead.

"What happened?" he asked.

I moved back so he could see into the freezer.

"What the fuck," he said. He took a step closer. "That's so fucked up. That's the weirdest fucking thing I've ever seen." He started laughing too. "Do you think they killed it like that?"

"Oh my god, no," I said. "Who would do that? It might have been dead before they put it in the freezer."

"How the fuck are we going to get this thing out?"

I was nearly crying. "I don't fucking know!"

"I dare you to touch it."

"No fucking way. I dare *you* to touch it."

He took another step closer, and before I could react, Noah grabbed my arm and shoved my hand into the freezer toward the frozen cat. Individual hairs broke off as my fist collided with the scruff of its neck.

Noah released me and broke away, laughing hysterically. I stared at my arm in the freezer until my vision tunnelled, then grabbed a small handful of shards of hair and flung them at his face.

He coughed and spat. "That went in my fucking mouth."

I realized I'd miscalculated. "Oh god, I'm sorry, I meant that as a joke—I didn't mean—" But then Noah pinned me front-first to the fridge with his body. His hand snaked over the back of my skull and pulled out the elastic that held my ponytail in place. My dark brown hair fell over my face in sweaty strings. He shoved my head into the freezer so I came face to face with the tabby.

"See how it feels?" he said.

I pinched my eyes and mouth shut. A nervous giggle pushed against the back of my teeth and bubbled back down into my throat.

"Do you like that?"

I wanted to be violent but I didn't know how. I couldn't move. I remembered my sister's advice.

I let my lips part, just a fraction of an inch.

His groin pressed into the top of my ass. I could feel his erection through his jeans and my yoga pants. "Do you like that, Nah-tah-lee-ah?" Noah said again.

My chin ached where it had scraped against the ice. "Do you?" I said.

It worked. Noah released my head and spun me around so that I was still pinned against the fridge, but now we were face to face. If I were Sara, I thought, I'd—But I didn't know what Sara would do. I wasn't Sara.

"Please let me go," I said gently.

He stared at me. I could feel him—all of him—against me.

"Noah," I said again. "Let me go."

He blinked and nodded slightly. I felt his grip loosen.

Then Noah was pried off of me with a force that knocked me to my knees. Jeremy flung Noah across the room. He landed in an awkward crouch and scrambled to his feet just in time for Jeremy to punch him straight in the face. "She said to let her go!"

Noah crumbled to the ground and blood began to pour from his nose, which hung crooked. "Jeremy, holy shit, Jeremy, stop," I said. I grabbed the back of his T-shirt both to hold him back and pull myself up. "I'm fine."

We heard a muffled groan. On the floor, Noah held both hands over his nose, blood and mucus seeping through his fingers.

"I think we need to take him to a hospital."

Tears pooled at the bottom of Noah's eyes.

"Jeremy? Jer? Do we have an ice pack? We should go."

Jeremy nudged Noah with the toe of his massive boot, then turned around and stuck both hands in the freezer and ripped out the cat, leaving most of its hair behind.

He dropped it on the floor next to Noah with a clunk, and then walked out of the room and out of the house. As he left, I heard him say, "Ungrateful bitch."

Peter had come downstairs at some point during all of this, and after Jeremy left, he helped Noah up, and we walked him outside only to discover that Jeremy had left with one of the vans. I told Peter to take the second one to the hospital. "I'm going to bus home," I said.

Peter nodded. A trail of Noah's blood wandered down his shirt, but he didn't seem to notice. "What about the job?" he said.

"What about it? I'm quitting. Jeremy and Noah can explain."

Noah clambered up and into the passenger's seat, his head tilted down. He picked up a hoodie from the floor and held it to his face. Peter climbed in the driver's side and they drove away.

Later, when I told Sara what had happened, she clenched her fists until her knuckles turned white, and said, "I'll fucking kill him. Both of them maybe." Rage had always looked good on Sara. Her eyes were vibrant and intense. Her skin glowed.

"No, you won't," I said.

"I'll beat him within an inch of death."

"I'm fine, Sara, I'm fine. It wasn't that big a deal. Besides," I said, "I started it."

Sara looked at me for a long time. I couldn't read her expression, but it made me want to sink so far into her sofa, I disappeared.

Finally, she spoke. "If that's a narrative you can live with."

I told her I didn't understand, and she told me I would when I was older. And true to her word, one day I was older, and I understood.

FROM A
HIGH PLACE

After university, Emma and I moved to an overpriced and under-square-footed apartment on the hipster (i.e., moderately less expensive) fringe of downtown Vancouver to try to break into the film industry. She immediately got a job as a production assistant on a popular TV show through the father of a friend of a friend, while I bounced between internships and fucked around with a screenplay until, eight months later, I landed a communications job at an art-house theatre that doubled as the headquarters for Canada's second-largest film festival, updating the website and social media, and sending out weekly e-newsletters with film listings. "Basically," I explained to Emma over celebratory drinks at the end of my first week, "I'm a cut-and-paste technician." I was required to do few tasks that involved actual communication skills or knowledge of independent film. Still, I was twenty-three and making 36k plus extended benefits in *Vancouver* in the *arts*.

"We're living the dream," Emma said, raising her pint. "I love it. Rhee? I love being on set." She leaned in. "So you know that guy I was talking about, Will? The assistant cameraman? The cute one, with the eyebrow ring and the hair. We talked again the other day, we're becoming *friends*. I'm just waiting for an opportunity, when it isn't awkward, or too awkward, and I'll be like *how did you get your job?"* Emma's game plan was to become a cinematographer. It was the basis of our friendship— I wrote and directed, she shot. Before moving to Vancouver, we'd made five student films together, two of which had screened in small to mid-size festivals across the country. We wanted to make more films, but by moving we'd cut our post-secondary umbilical cord; without easy access to equipment, an editing suite, and an endless supply of eager film and theatre students, we didn't know where to start. Still, we were confident that this was the beginning of *figuring it out*.

I tapped her glass with mine. "Cheers."

One month later she confessed that she hated her job, and maybe this wasn't the career she wanted. She hated the hours, hated the assistant director—"Which one?" I asked. "All of them," she said—hated all the standing and waiting, and she'd just read on *Indiewire* that only two per cent of Hollywood cinematographers were female. Visions of Emma shattering the glass ceiling were replaced with visions of Emma as a bug crushed against a windshield. We could both see it (she was good, but was she *two per cent* good?), and after another month she convinced her boss to lay her off and went on unemployment. She set up a portfolio site and tried to make it as a wedding photographer, but had a rough go of it. In Vancouver, there are more photographers than weddings. She started sleeping in late and watching hours of sitcoms. She used the word *ennui* a lot, but that was nothing new.

Our apartment was on the twelfth floor and faced southwest, overlooking three blocks of low-rise rental buildings. The building was the same age as our grandparents. A concrete thumb poking up from the city. The rooms in the suites jutted out of the building as half octagons and the walls met at the front door. Our two-bedroom suite, I liked to joke, was shaped like a three-breasted woman.

"Maybe in a cartoon," Emma said.

"Yeah, like if Jessica Rabbit had a third breast, in the middle." I pointed to my own chest.

She laughed the first time and so I drove that joke into the ground. When she got quiet or awkward or was rewatching *The Mindy Project* for the tenth time and I began to get worried, I'd make a joke like, "I'll be in Jessica Rabbit's left boob, knock if you need me."

I came home from work one day in late June to find all the furniture in Jessica Rabbit's middle boob stacked on the couch near the front entrance, except for my two bookshelves, which had been dragged against two of the six walls of my bedroom, and the television, which had been relocated to the right boob, next to Emma's bed.

"The fuck?"

"You're always watching Netflix on your computer anyway, but if you want, we can move the TV in with you," Emma said. She was crouched in front of an elaborate diorama made of plasticine, construction paper, canvas, yarn, pipe cleaners, and other dollar-store items. She positioned her camera close to one scene, her neck stretched out and her eyes pinched. She moved the camera less than a centimetre every time she adjusted it. Emma had an eye for angles, for details. Even unemployed, she was obsessed with aesthetics, always stylishly dressed and wearing light makeup, whereas on a good day I showed up at work in what is best described as "business grunge."

"It's fine," I said. I peered down over her shoulder as she snapped a photo.

The camera was focused on a model of a living room. A plasticine doll sat on a couch and watched a blank piece of turquoise construction paper on a plasticine television. "I'm going to green-screen something in later," Emma explained.

"Is this a film?"

"Yeah." She moved the character's arm by a hair, took another picture.

"What's it about?"

"How we're willing to destroy ourselves to be loved."

"Okay."

"Mm."

I watched her for a bit, until it became awkward. "Well," I said. "I'm going to go hang out in Jessica Rabbit's left nipple. Knock if you need me."

"God, shut up," she said. "Do you even know what boobs look like?"

The summer heat turned into a summer heat wave. The sun burned through our floor-to-ceiling windows and cooked our apartment. Emma's cast and set began to melt in her fingers.

"You could just work it into the plot," I suggested. She threw a cushion at me.

Emma opened all five windows as wide as they would open—less than the width of a starfished hand—and replaced my pink curtains in the living room with thick white linen. We didn't have air conditioning, so I bought three fans and put one in each breast. Emma was worried that the fans would knock over a character or prop and wreck her continuity, so I had to face all three away from her, not that they made much of a difference to the temperature anyway—they only churned the hot air around the apartment.

We both slept in our underwear, with our blankets and sheets in balls on the floor, and our bedroom doors open.

"Have you lost weight?" I asked as she stretched one morning.

"I've been going to the gym," she said.

"When?"

"When you're at work."

"Are you eating?"

"Of course I'm fucking eating."

"That's good."

She glared at me.

"I mean, that you're leaving the house. Um. Exercising. I should go to the gym more." I pinched my bicep, which was noticeably flabbier than it had been a year ago. Since starting at the theatre I'd gained five pounds and a persistent muscle knot next to my right shoulder blade that sometimes caused tension headaches.

"Stop staring, it's weirding me out." She stuck her tongue out at me and closed the door.

When I got home that evening, the long sliding panes from four of our five windows were stacked on the couch. The whole apartment buzzed with the white noise of city life: wheels grinding against pavement, pedestrian conversation, buskers and car radios blasting music. I found Emma in her bedroom, watching *Planet Earth*, the volume high. It was noticeably cooler with the windows gone, and for the first time in a week she was wearing more than a tank top and a pair of lady briefs.

"Aren't you worried about the wind?" I asked.

She looked up and paused her show with the remote. "Hey!" She bounced out of bed. "Check it out! Isn't it so much better in here?"

"Yeah," I said. "But what about your film?"

"What about it?"

"Won't the wind knock things over?"

"Nah, I finished my scene. Going to wait 'til it cools down before I start the next one. I put all the characters in a Tupperware." She pointed to a large plastic container on her desk. "Isn't this great? I got the idea from one of our neighbours. I was out—getting groceries—and I looked up and saw that someone had taken their windows out and I was like, whoa, now there's a solution. I left yours in, but I can show you how to take it out, if you'd like."

"No!" I said. "Thanks."

"Suit yourself." She walked around her bed to the window.

A bubble of anguish squeezed its way up my windpipe and out of my mouth.

Emma glanced over her shoulder at me. "What was *that*?"

"Be careful," I repeated. I realized my hand was stretched out to catch her.

"Be careful of *what*? The window?" she said. "I'm not going to fall out of the window, Rhiannon, I'm not a toddler."

"It's big enough to fall out of. You could trip," I added. "Or roll off the bed and out." I demonstrated with my hands, stabbing my fingers downward to animate the fall.

Emma shook her head, then suddenly she tipped back manically like she was about to take a pratfall out the window. I opened my mouth but no sound came out. At the last second, she shot her arms out and caught herself on the wall and the remaining pane. "It would have to be *very* catastrophic," she said, laughing.

"Jesus fucking Christ."

"Don't be such a pussy."

"Seriously, Emma. Put them back in. This freaks me out."

"It's my window."

"Yeah, well, we share the ones in the living room."

Emma looked at me and slowly nodded. "Okay, fine. I'll put those back in. But you're being ridiculous."

"I'm not being ridiculous, there are enormous holes in our walls, then a twelve-storey drop! What if an earthquake threw you out of one? What if you got drunk? What if you were to sleepwalk?" I picked up speed as I spoke; I could feel my face turn red from exertion. "You have to put yours back in too."

"What if an *earthquake*—"

"We live in an earthquake zone! That's why I don't hang framed pictures above my bed!"

She looked at me like I was psychotic. I felt a little psychotic, so the way she was looking at me made perfect sense.

I was gripped by an irrational sort of fear I couldn't quite twist into words. Emma was right—the opening was less than two feet wide; it was very unlikely one of us would accidentally fall through and plummet to her death. *I'll show you who's a pussy*, I thought, and I imagined myself vaulting over Emma's bed and diving out the window. By the time she realized what was happening, there'd just be the soles of my feet and my flexed toes, and then the sound of my body splitting open, my bones splintering, my organs bursting like...water balloons?—I studied film and general arts at university, I don't know how bodies burst—the screams, then the sirens, and the swooshing sound of photos uploaded to social media. #Splat.

I took a huge step back, so I was under the door frame. Then I turned and walked to the middle of the living room, where I stood for twenty minutes, my arms crossed and sweaty, my foot tapping like a drummer, staring down, godlike, at the little world Emma had created in our apartment while on the other side of it she slowly reattached the windowpanes. When she finished, she reopened the three windows as far as they would go, less than the width of my hand.

The fall before we graduated, Emma had a bad case of the sads, as she called it, and told me she didn't want to be alive anymore. "I don't want to kill myself," she said. "I just don't want to continue living. There's a difference."

Is there? I wondered. I spent an hour counting all the things Emma had to live for, until she booted me out of the house she shared with three of her friends. "I fucking know,

Rhee. I fucking know all this. You're making it worse. You need to go."

Nearly two years later, the incident still rattled me. I'd known Emma five years and had begun to think of her as a brilliant but loose light bulb, forever flickering between the most amazing light and consuming darkness. When she was happy, she was radiant, magnetic. But when she tipped into black moods, she pushed people away (sometimes literally, with her hands), her face all shadows like there was a cloud above her head that only she could see and be shaded by. Still, before that night, Emma had never said anything to me that suggested her delicate moods were more than lingering adolescent angst mixed with an artistic temperament. *I don't want to be alive anymore.* You don't just forget shit like that, when you care about someone.

I started making up excuses to text Emma while I was at work. *Hey do we have toilet paper? If not I'll get some. Want to get sushi for dinner tonight? What's our postal code again I'm filling out a form. I just emailed you about a cool job did you get it?*

Her responses left little room to continue the conversation. *We're low awesome see you tonight. Sure! Google it fuckwit. Yep thanks.*

I kept one hand on my phone as I clicked-and-dragged, copied-and-pasted, and waited for her to text me back.

It wasn't that I worried she was currently suicidal—not entirely. But when I went to work the morning after Emma removed her window, it occurred to me that if I came home and learned she had gone out the window, I would never know whether she jumped or fell, and *then* I started thinking about whether it was worse for someone to accidentally or deliberately fall to their death. On the one hand, if it was an accident, there was nothing we could do to prevent it, but she would have died when she wanted to live. On the other hand, if it was deliberate, we would obsess over how we could have helped, how we could have saved her, but she would have died because she didn't want to be alive anymore. Or was it that the sads prevented her from realizing she wanted to live? I went back and forth on this for days, googled article after article about depression and suicidal thoughts, and in the end the only thing I knew for sure was that not knowing would drive me insane.

How we're willing to destroy ourselves to be loved.

I asked her what she meant.

"When did I say that?" she said.

"When I asked you what your film's about."

"Oh," she said. "I meant it literally. It's about a person who physically destroys herself for love. Like, takes herself apart. It's a claymation," she explained, like you would to a child.

"Is it about Alex?" Alex was her ex. They'd broken up just over two years ago, before Emma's last bad case of the sads.

"No," she said. "It's just a story. Is every story you write about someone you know?"

"No," I lied.

Across the room, the window taunted us with its open mouth.

July came and went and the sun continued to throb. The local newspapers encouraged citizens to conserve water and ran weekly updates on forest fires in the Okanagan. "What a fucking dumb city," Emma said. "Spends ten months bitching about the rain, the other two freaking out about a drought."

I nodded. I couldn't imagine anyone staying in that apartment all day without popping like a kernel. My job was mind-numbing as fuck, but at least the office had air conditioning.

Emma grew impatient and decided to start shooting her next scene, fuck the heat. The set expanded to take up most of Jessica Rabbit's middle breast. She left me a narrow path from my bedroom to the kitchen to the front door, but Emma had to climb over the couch—and her discarded window-pane—to get in and out of her own room.

It hardly mattered: as the days grew shorter, my work hours stretched longer and I spent less time at home. Festival madness was upon us. The staff quadrupled; contractors were brought on board and took over a chunk of my year-round responsibilities (all the ones that required even an iota of brain activity). I copied-and-pasted text from emails into our website, and text from our film database into MailChimp, eight, then nine, then ten hours a day plus weekends. I started to give zero shits when I saw spelling or grammatical errors. When my officemate was out, I closed the door and watched Vimeo screeners of festival films in a small window in the corner of my monitor while copying-and-pasting. It only slowed me down a little.

On my lunch break, I tried to teach myself French using an iPhone app because I thought it might make me more employable. *Qui habite dans le château?* Who lives in the castle? *C'est une nouvelle frontière.* It is a new border. *Tu n'es pas à ta place ici.* You do not belong here. I screen-captured the last one and sent it to Emma in a text message.

She responded immediately. *Et toi, Duolingo?*

Il sait. Il dit la vérité.

Lol.

I stared at my phone for minutes, trying to think of a way to continue the conversation, but then my bento box was ready and I took it back to the theatre to eat it at my desk.

When, after forty-seven days, the sun finally quit, it quit with a vengeance. I stared out the window with my office-mate and the communications intern we'd picked up in late July as wind and rain tore at the building; we watched hungrily for lightning after every groan of thunder. "It's not dark enough to see it," Marie said, after a while. "But I bet it's there." It was nearly 8:00 p.m.

I didn't have an umbrella or a coat, so I hugged the sides of buildings as I rushed home through the city core. I was soaked through to my underwear within a block. Every few minutes I stopped to check the sky. I wondered what it felt like to be hit by lightning. Though I realized, peering up between the buildings, that if it were going to happen it probably wouldn't happen while I was standing in the middle of downtown Vancouver, at sea level, since lightning always strikes the highest place. Then again, I thought I remembered reading somewhere that that was a myth. Probably on the internet.

When I opened the door to our apartment, I was dismayed to see Emma's windowpane still propped up on the couch.

"Emma?" I said. I didn't expect an answer. She must have left before the storm hit. I could see her curtains billowing into her bedroom, the foot of her comforter dark with rainwater.

I climbed over the couch—carefully, so I didn't drip on the sprawling film set—then reached back to pick up the windowpane. It was heavier than I expected and I had to take a step to steady myself before I could spin around to dump it on Emma's bed. I inched my way toward the window and cautiously pulled the curtains apart. Cars streaked past on the street below. No sign of Emma, I noted, and then felt ashamed. I wondered how far I could propel myself if I jumped—could I make it to the roof of the low-rise across the street? Or could I even make it past the driveway of our building's parking garage? The storm spat at me with contempt.

I tried to think back to when Emma had replaced the three living room windows. How did it go in? I glanced back at the bed. Which side was up? I felt nauseated. Why was I trying to help Emma anyway? She was the one stupid enough to leave a gaping hole in her bedroom in the middle of a rainstorm. She wasn't home, so she'd obviously accepted the consequences. I realized I was crying. Why was I crying? I sat back heavily on my ass. Fuck this. No one was making me solve Emma's problems for her. I didn't have to do anything. I stood up and rushed out of her room. As I cleared the couch, I felt something soft and cool beneath my bare foot. I'd stepped on one of the houses from the film set. I peeled the muddied plasticine off my foot and carried it back into Emma's room. I sat on her bed, my ass against the windowpane, and sobbed onto the handful of clay.

I don't know how long I sat there for before I heard the door. I looked up from my knees as Emma climbed over the couch to her bedroom. "Rhee? You're home! Oh my fucking god, this storm, eh? Is my shit okay?"

I nodded, dully. Really, what harm can a little water do?

"What's wrong?"

"I'm so sorry," I said.

"What? What is it?"

"I stepped on one of your houses." I held up the handful of clay. "The one near the door."

"Oh," Emma said. "Oh my god, don't cry. I can make a new one."

"I wrecked the continuity."

"No, no you didn't. I didn't start shooting that bit yet. It's okay."

"I was trying to figure out how to put the window back."

"It's really easy. Look." She picked up the windowpane and stepped around me to lodge it back in place, inserting it into the top groove first, then jamming it back on the bottom track. She tested it. It slid open easily. She closed it again. "Thanks for trying," she said. "I know you're scared of heights."

"Yeah," I said. "I thought I was going to puke."

"Oh gross, can you image if that landed on someone?"

"Hah, what's the velocity of falling vomit? Depends on the size of the chunks, right?"

"No, size doesn't matter. Physics, yo."

"Sure."

"Rhee? Don't cry. Seriously, it's not a big deal. It's not like you stepped on the protagonist."

I nodded dully. "I'm okay. It's just the rain."

"I read this article the other day," Emma said, sinking down next to me on the bed. "About something called the high-place phenomenon. It's the urge to jump or thoughts about jumping when you're standing in a high place looking down. It's super-common. Apparently it's the reason a lot of people are scared of heights."

"Oh," I said.

"I get it all the time. Like, I look down, and I think, what if I jumped?" She laughed. "Maybe I'll fly. Only one way to find out."

"One hundred per cent," I said. "You won't fly. Physics, yo." I made an awkward gangster-like sign with my free hand and smirked.

"Are you sure you're okay?" Emma said. "Your eyes are red."

"Yeah," I said. "I'm fine. I'm just tired." I dropped my head onto her shoulder.

She rested her head on mine and ran her fingers through my hair. I pressed the plasticine between my palms, again and again, until all the colours bled into one.

I WAS MADE TO LOVE YOU

BY EMMA MORRISON

INT. BLUE'S APARTMENT—LIVING ROOM

BLUE—an ageless, androgynous nude person made of light blue plasticine, except for their eyes, which are white with black pupils, and their mouth, which is black—sits on a sofa, watching an old film. They balance a TV tray on their lap and eat their dinner.

In the film, a man sits on a bar stool next to a woman. He orders drinks from the bartender by lifting two fingers. The woman smiles.

BLUE turns off the TV. They look at the empty spot on the couch.

They blink and frown, their eyes sad.

INT. BLUE'S APARTMENT—KITCHEN

BLUE scrapes food off their dish into a garbage can. They fill a kettle with water, boil it on the stovetop. As the water boils, they mash their plate into a ball of white plasticine, then reshape it into a mug. They drop a tea bag into the mug and fill it with water from the kettle. They hear LAUGH-TER. They wander to the kitchen window and look down at the street.

EXT. STREET—EVENING

BROWN and GREEN walk hand in hand. GREEN kisses BROWN on the cheek. They leave their lips behind after the kiss.

BROWN pulls the lips off their face and puts them back on GREEN.

GREEN laughs.

INT. BLUE'S APARTMENT—KITCHEN

The sound of GREEN's laughter is cut off when BLUE SLAMS the window shut.

They look around the kitchen. Then back at the window.

BLUE grabs their wallet from the kitchen table. They dig their hand into their hip and open a pocket. They put the wallet inside and walk toward the front door.

INT. BAR—EVENING

BLUE enters the bar. There are a few plasticine people scattered in pairs and small groups, but they are the only one who is alone.

They sit at the bar and order a drink.

PURPLE walks past BLUE to the bathroom. BLUE smiles. PURPLE doesn't notice.

The BARTENDER brings BLUE their drink. They take a sip, tap their fingers, look around the bar. They fail to make eye contact.

Then: the front doors swing open. YELLOW walks in, alone, bathed in light. All eyes turn to stare and follow them as they walk into the bar and take an empty seat one over from BLUE.

BLUE stares at YELLOW. Their hand trembles.

BLUE inhales deeply. They hop over to the seat next to YELLOW.

YELLOW looks at BLUE. BLUE smiles at YELLOW and lifts two fingers at the BARTENDER.

YELLOW shakes their head and turns their back to BLUE.

BLUE rushes to the bathroom. THEY bump into PURPLE, on their way out.

INT. BAR—BATHROOM

BLUE stares into the mirror. They rub their face, blending wrinkles into smoother skin. They pick up the corners of their mouth to create a smile. It's creepy. They frown.

INT. BAR—EVENING

PURPLE is sitting next to YELLOW, flirting. PURPLE orders two drinks.

BLUE grimaces but returns to the bar to pay their tab. They pull out their wallet aggressively and a chunk of their hip rips off and falls to the ground.

PURPLE looks down and sees BLUE's hip on the floor. They laugh. BLUE drops a bill on the bar, scoops up their hip, and walks quickly out of the bar.

INT. BLUE'S APARTMENT

BLUE re-enters their apartment, the chunk of their hip still in their hands.

They start to reattach the chunk to their body, then pause. They hold it up and mush it into a small ball. They pinch out a bit in the front to form a nose.

BLUE's eyes light up. They smile.

INT. BLUE'S APARTMENT—KITCHEN

BLUE sits at their kitchen table, pulling small handfuls of plasticine from their body and adding them to their sculpture.

They mould it into a head and face that looks very similar to their own.

They pull off their mouth and rip it in half. They put half the mouth back on their face and the other half on the head.

They pull their left eye off and add it to the head.

Beat. The head—BLUE2—winks and smiles at BLUE.

BLUE is delighted. They cradle BLUE2 to their chest.

SERIES OF SHOTS WITH HAPPY MUSIC:

INT. BLUE'S APARTMENT—LIVING ROOM

BLUE watches a movie with BLUE2 on their lap. They both smile at the same time when the on-screen couple kisses.

EXT. STREET—DAY

BLUE bikes along the street, with BLUE2 in the basket.

EXT. PARK—DAY

BLUE and BLUE2 at the park. BLUE holds BLUE2 in both hands and they spin, facing each other, laughing.

INT. BAR—EVENING

BLUE and BLUE2 at the bar. BLUE rests BLUE2 on the bar top, and BLUE2 starts to roll off.

The MUSIC slows.

BLUE catches BLUE2 before they hit the ground. Both look terrified.

BLUE scrapes some more plasticine off their body and builds BLUE2 a neck. They put BLUE2 back on the bar top, and this time they don't fall.

The drinks arrive.

BLUE inserts a straw into BLUE2's mouth. Both smile.

INT. BLUE'S APARTMENT—BEDROOM—NIGHT

BLUE carries BLUE2 into the bedroom and places them on a pillow. BLUE tucks themself into bed.

BLUE rolls over and their arm smacks the mattress where BLUE2's body should be.

BLUE grabs their pillow and puts it on the mattress below BLUE2's head. They hug the pillow.

BLUE frowns and opens their eye. They glance at BLUE2, who has opened their eye and is staring back at BLUE. BLUE2 winks. BLUE winks.

BLUE sits up. They pull a handful of plasticine from their body and look at it.

INT. BLUE'S APARTMENT—BEDROOM—NIGHT—LATER

BLUE—now significantly smaller than before—finishes moulding BLUE2's torso.

BLUE2 bends up to kiss BLUE on the cheek.

BLUE smiles.

They curl up in bed together, and BLUE drapes their arm over BLUE2.

Night turns into day.

BLUE and BLUE2 wake up.

BLUE struggles to lift BLUE2 out of bed. They waddle out the door.

INT. BLUE'S APARTMENT—KITCHEN

BLUE places BLUE2 on a chair at the kitchen table.

They drop a bowl of cereal and a spoon in front of them.

BLUE sits down across from BLUE2 with their own bowl. They take a few bites.

BLUE2 looks down at the bowl, then face-plants into it to try to eat. They knock the bowl off the table.

BLUE looks up and sees the bowl on the floor. BLUE2 looks sheepish.

BLUE stands up. They pick the cereal bowl off the floor.

They drop the bowl, full again, in front of BLUE2.

BLUE rips their left arm off and attaches it to the left side of BLUE2's body.

BLUE2 picks up the spoon carefully. They take a bite, then look up at BLUE, smiling.

When BLUE2's bowl is empty, BLUE tries to pick them up, but is unable to.

BLUE looks at their legs, then at the table.

They flip the table and break off two legs.

They attach one to BLUE2's body.

BLUE removes their right leg and attaches the table leg to their own body in its place.

They attach their leg to the right side of BLUE2's body.

BLUE holds out their hand to BLUE2 to pull them up.

BLUE2 stumbles but catches themself.

BLUE kisses BLUE2. BLUE2 kicks their new right leg.

EXT. STREET—DAY

BLUE and BLUE2 step outside their building.

They hobble down the street side by side, so their arms are in and their legs are out.

BLUE reaches to take BLUE2's hand.

INT. BAR—EVENING

BLUE and BLUE2 sit together in the bar. BLUE offers BLUE2 a bite of their burger. BLUE2 shakes their head. They hold one finger up, then stand and walk toward the bathroom.

INT. BAR—BATHROOM

BLUE2 looks at themself in the mirror: one-eyed, one-armed, one-legged, and so thin they can barely stand.

A toilet FLUSHES.

YELLOW comes out of a stall and washes their hands.

BLUE2 ogles YELLOW.

YELLOW glances at BLUE2. They giggle, cover their mouth, and leave the bathroom.

BLUE2 slams their hand down on the sink. They try to rip the towel dispenser from the wall, but they aren't strong enough, so they start tearing the towels down and throwing them onto the floor until there are none left.

INT. BLUE'S APARTMENT—BEDROOM—NIGHT

BLUE and BLUE2 sleep side by side, BLUE's arm slung over BLUE2. BLUE2 lifts BLUE's arm and sits up. BLUE continues to sleep. BLUE2 looks at their body.

They reach over and scrape plasticine from BLUE's body. BLUE doesn't wake up.

BLUE2 adds the plasticine to their own body.

BLUE2 trails a finger along BLUE's face, down their neck, to their shoulder. They rip off BLUE's arm.

BLUE's eye opens. They see BLUE2 holding their arm, sit up, and SCREAM.

BLUE2 attaches the arm to their body.

With both arms, they reach for BLUE.

INT. BLUE'S APARTMENT—KITCHEN

BLUE2 sits at the repaired kitchen table, eating cereal. Their body is fuller and they have two legs, two arms, two eyes, a full mouth.

Their left eye is lopsided. It falls off and lands in the cereal bowl.

BLUE2 picks it up and puts it back on their face.

INT. BAR—EVENING

BLUE2 sits at the bar with a drink, their eyes on the door.

Then: the front doors swing open. YELLOW walks in alone, bathed in a glowing light. All eyes turn to look at them, following them as they walk into the bar and take an empty seat one over from BLUE2.

BLUE2 stares at YELLOW. Their hand trembles.

BLUE2 inhales deeply. They hop over to the seat next to YELLOW.

YELLOW looks at BLUE2. BLUE2 smiles at YELLOW and lifts two fingers at the BARTENDER.

FADE TO BLACK

THE MANDRAKE

Angelina and Rick had been trying to conceive for three years when he brought a mandrake home from the university. "Mandragora." He pronounced each syllable. Angelina weighed the plant in her hands—the base of the pot was as wide as a dinner plate and heavy leaves spilled over the rim. "Mandrake."

"Like in *Harry Potter*?"

"Sure, not that they did much with it." He stared at her.

Angelina shook her head. "I don't get it."

"Think Donne—*Go and catch a falling star/Get with child a mandrake root*—"

She thrust the pot back into his hands. "What the fuck? Is this some sort of joke?"

He placed the mandrake on their kitchen counter. "Yeah, relax, it's a joke," he said. "I mean, it's also sort of meant as a good-luck charm, in a we-know-it's-bogus-mythology kind of way, it's just because the root kind of looks like a fetus, which you can't see, because it's in the ground, but—"

"So you went out and bought a plant?"

"No, we had some in the greenhouse, and I had a grad student pot this one. I thought—"

"There's no way you were thinking."

"—I thought you'd find it funny."

Angelina thumbed a hangnail, then pinched it so it bled.

Rick shoved his hands into the pockets of his brown slacks. "I'm sorry?" he asked. He sounded sincere and even a little sad, which surprised Angelina. The gift was classic Rick—the sort of thing he normally would apologize for with a loaded clarification. *I'm sorry you're upset.*

Angelina had met Rick eleven years earlier in a History of Biology seminar at the University of Toronto, which he was teaching as a PhD student. She was in the final year of a useless psychology major and had taken the course for an easy science credit. It was, she'd speculated, much easier to understand and discuss the *implications* of science than science itself. She later bailed on her plans to pursue a PhD, got her MLIS instead, and now worked at the Vancouver Public Library.

Rick was more interested in theory than practice, the sort of man who quoted Galen and Aristotle and Hippocrates but couldn't perform CPR or trim a hedge. In recent years, his passion had shifted almost entirely to cryptozoology, a field of study that involved far less travel and far more reading than Angelina had initially suspected. He'd taken a position as a lecturer in the Faculty of Arts at UBC, where he taught undergraduate philosophy and biology courses and occasionally mentored eccentric master's students who went diving in the Okanagan to look for Ogopogo and wrote dissertations on the mythologies of the lotus tree. He had no chance of a promotion. Sometimes, in her head and never out loud, Angelina joked that she'd found a man with the arrogance but not the paycheque of a professor.

Later that day, Angelina side-eyed Rick through their bedroom window while he toiled awkwardly away in their small backyard, his glasses slipping down his nose and the seat of his slacks tight over his ass as he hunched on his heels and tenderly patted down the dirt around his goddamn mandrake. Angelina half-expected the root to scream (she knew *some* bits of mandrake lore, thank you very much), and she was disappointed to see it was a fairly typical-looking taproot. Angelina couldn't see the resemblance to a fetus or a child at all.

She went downstairs and found Rick rinsing his hands over the sink. He smiled when she brushed dirt from the bridge of his nose. "I'm cursed now, you know," he said. "It's said that if you uproot a mandrake, you're doomed to go to hell."

Angelina decided to humour him. "Perhaps you're forgiven when you put it back in the ground."

He kissed her then, and as they kissed she pretended she couldn't feel the chilly emptiness growing in her gut and her heart.

As he pulled away, he kept his hands on her shoulders.

When Rick and Angelina first got together, the sex had been passionate and frequent. Angelina had only had one partner before Rick—an ex-boyfriend who at nineteen had been a virgin too. Rick was seven years older, and he was generous with those extra years of experience. He massaged knots out of her shoulders as he pressed into her. He knew the perfect place to kiss her neck. He pounced on her so quickly (and, often, drunkenly—but they were both students, both young), she sometimes found him inside her before she could remind him to use a condom—so she went on the pill. Once Angelina graduated and they went public with the relationship, Rick kept at least one hand touching her wherever they went. She felt irresistible.

But lately there had been something stilted about their lovemaking, as though by introducing functionality they had drained the act of passion. The more Angelina worried about it, the more awkward it became, and she could tell that Rick was worried too.

Since she had stopped taking birth control and started waiting (and waiting and waiting), Angelina's sleep had been disturbed with anxious, self-deprecating thoughts and vivid nightmares that left her lonely and covered in cold sweat. She had wondered, briefly, if she was going through premature menopause, but multiple trips to the doctor had found nothing physically wrong with either her or Rick (*physically!* she extrapolated—what, then, underlay it all?). She sat in the bathroom longer than she needed to, peeling the skin under her fingernails off with tweezers.

It only happened once, they told her—Rick had taken Maria, the graduate student, to the campus bar for a drink to talk about potential thesis topics. She had written in her personal statement that she was interested in studying the implications of the possible (but unproven) medicinal properties of the silphium seed, an extinct plant rumoured to be the origin of the "heart" symbol.

"It might have been a contraceptive," Maria said. It was ten days after Rick's confession, and the three of them were in Rick and Angelina's living room, the two of them drinking beer, and Maria drinking Coca-Cola. "But really, I didn't have my argument. I had an example for an argument. We were talking about religious oppression, but I wasn't getting anywhere *concrete*. I don't think I'm going to write about that anymore." Her mouth twisted in self-awareness. After hours of fruitless conversation, Maria explained, she and Rick had drowned their frustrations past the point of reason and it was in this state they found themselves on the couch in Maria's basement suite.

Rick often came home tasting like beer, but rarely drunk. "When was this?" Angelina asked.

"Seven weeks ago," Maria said. "A Thursday, I think."

Her story matched Rick's. Angelina sighed.

"It only happened once," Rick said. "One time in eleven years, Angelina. I'm so sorry."

"I should have known," she said. "You always had a thing for younger women."

He smiled. "You'll always be a younger woman."

"Fuck you, Rick."

"You know I love you. You're my unicorn." He hung his head and peered up at her through strands of greying hair, his hands grabbing and releasing fistfuls of his shirt, his left knee twitching anxiously. Angelina wanted to put a hand on it to still it.

When Rick went outside to smoke, Maria said, "Unicorn?"

Angelina watched through the glass door as he walked down the steps and padded barefoot onto the yard to flick ashes onto the dirt. "Yep," she said. "Unicorn. On one of our first dates, I asked him what his favourite animal was and he said it was the unicorn. He told me that men spent years searching for unicorns, how stories mutated to create the myth. A typo here, an exaggeration there, a narwhal horn here..."

When she looked back, Maria had both hands clasped around her drink and was taking frequent nervous sips.

"Marco Polo tried to track down unicorns in India," Angelina said, "but all he found was an Indian rhinoceros. He was pretty disappointed by how ugly 'unicorns' turned out to be. Rick said when he first saw me, the first time I showed up at office hours, he felt as though he'd stumbled across something rare and mystical that he'd been searching for forever. That I was his unicorn."

"Oh. That's sweet."

"Not really," Angelina said. "When you think about it."

Maria pressed her lips together. After a moment, she nodded and said, "Yeah."

With the introduction of a new symbol in her life, Angelina's nightmares had mutated from prosaic to mystical. Every night for the last ten days she had dreamed of walking through a field of enormous mandrakes. She stopped at each plant and pulled on the stubborn leaves until they cut the flesh between her fingers. Finally, at the last plant, the leaves broke from the stem but left the root buried. As the massive leaves glided to the ground, she dropped to her knees and pressed an ear against the dirt, and every night for a week, she had woken up to the muted screams of a crying infant echoing in her bedroom, her fingertips bleeding from grinding into the headboard. Finally, on the ninth day, she had called Rick and told him he could come home. On one condition.

Angelina realized she was digging her fingers into her leg, the dull pain tingling up her arm and neck. When she pulled her hand away, she left spots of blood on her skirt. "Do you want another drink?" she said, reaching for Maria's glass.

Maria's hands jerked back. "It's okay," she said. "I'll get it." She came back with a full Coke and two more beers, locked and crossed in her skinny fingers, the bottle caps removed. Her hands were shaking and the bottles clinked together again and again.

"Relax," Angelina said, accepting a bottle. She realized, as Maria dropped it on the coffee table, that the second beer was for Rick. She took a deep drink.

"I can't," Maria said. "This is too surreal. I mean, you should hate me. I hate me right now, and I didn't even know he was married when we—"

Angelina finished her beer and grabbed the one meant for Rick. "You didn't have to call attention to it," she said. "Get up, I want to show you something."

Angelina took Maria upstairs to the second bedroom, which, a year earlier, she had painted yellow and filled with IKEA furniture, stuffed animals, teething toys, and board books by her favourite children's authors—Robert Munsch,

Oliver Jeffers, Mem Fox, and others. She and Rick had spent a weekend assembling the crib, dresser, nightstand, and bookshelves, bolts and screws rolling around the hardwood floors, finding their way underneath their feet and knees and the palms of their hands. Angelina had placated Rick with kind words and self-deprecating jokes, but she had done most of the work. It made her angry and nostalgic and sad all at once, to think about all those times she'd calmed Rick's insecurities by placing herself and all of her skills and accomplishments beneath him, because she loved him, and maybe, a small, easy-to-dismiss part of her wondered, because she'd been with him since she was twenty-one and she didn't know any other ways to be in love.

"I thought you didn't have any children," Maria said—with her small voice, the final word came out more like a squeak.

"We don't."

Angelina turned around in surprise. She hadn't heard Rick come in. His arms were crossed and the faint smell of cigarettes permeated the air around him. She wanted to crawl inside his arms and press her face against his neck.

"We've been trying," he said.

"For how long?"

"Years." She pressed her fingernails into her arm. "And now there will be a baby?"

Maria paled and dropped a hand to her stomach.

Angelina's favourite animal was the rhinoceros. She could be just as pragmatic as Rick was fanciful. She sympathized with the Indian rhino. It must be hard to be constantly hunted down, only to be stared at with disappointment. It must be hard to be the reality when so many people have bought into the fantasy.

In their unborn child's bedroom, Angelina caught herself as she started to laugh and clamped her lips shut so she wouldn't spew beer onto the Winnie the Pooh rug. She felt something warm on the small of her back, and realized Rick was rubbing it. She swallowed. "I'm fine," she said. He withdrew his hand. The room wobbled like she was looking at it through water. She was a little drunk.

Maria looked paler than usual and her dark eyes were wide and wild. "Oh," she said, her hand massaging her abdomen.

Like she's going to rip it out, Angelina thought. "Excuse me," she said, pushing between Maria and Rick to leave the room before they could see the tears well in her eyes. She locked herself in the bathroom and pulled up her skirt and pulled down her underwear and pissed to cover up the noise she made sobbing into a hand towel. Her bladder went dry before her eyes so she washed her hands and stumbled down the stairs and made herself a rye and ginger and downed it in two gulps. She made another one to take upstairs.

As she rounded the stairs, she heard a choked sound, like a cough or a sob, and lingered on the landing, peering down the hall into the yellow bedroom. Rick and Maria spoke in whispers so quiet she could only understand their urgency, their faces so close and obscured by hair that their foreheads could be touching.

Angelina felt like an idiot. Why had she convinced herself that this could save them?

She slowly went back down the stairs. She stopped in the kitchen and stared at the countertop for a while, then stared at the stove and then the refrigerator, and she thought about how old the appliances were and how nice it would be to have newer ones, and maybe she should clean the appliances, because it would be something to do. But something and anything are different, she thought, while she finished her drink.

She meant to put her glass on the counter, but it missed and shattered on the floor. She stared at it, wiggling her bare toes between shards of glass, then crouched and picked up a larger piece and ran it under the nail of her index finger. She put her finger in her mouth and sucked, tasting blood. Except for the hum of the refrigerator and the grumble of the water heater, the house had gone silent. As she ran outside, a sharp pain in her foot told her she'd stepped on a piece of glass, but she kept running past the patio and down into the garden.

The mandrake was smaller than she remembered, and small buds she hadn't noticed before had gathered at its neck. She pried one open and plucked the beginning of a purple petal and put it on her tongue. She grabbed a handful of leaves and pulled, and the leaves broke off the plant, so she tossed them away and plunged her fingers into the dirt. Why, she wondered, in all those nights of dreaming had she not thought to just *dig*? The dirt was moist and cool and parted easily until she'd dug far enough down that she was able to pull the mandrake up from the earth at last. She held it up to the moonlight. It looked like an ordinary taproot.

Angelina dropped the mandrake into her lap and bent over, weeping, until her forehead nearly touched her knees. She stayed that way for a long time, and then she felt a hand on her shoulder. When she turned, Maria gazed down at her with sympathy, and Angelina almost buckled under the cruelty of the younger woman's kindness. Maria offered her hand and Angelina took it and let herself be pulled to her feet. The mandrake fell back to the ground. Rick waited, backlit and silhouetted in the sliding glass door, as Maria supported Angelina and helped her back across the garden and the patio and into the house.

NOSTALGIA

About halfway through my last summer at the pool, someone changed all the names on the shift schedule to Disney-themed nicknames. *Flounder 3–9 p.m. Monday, Wednesday, Saturday. Mufasa 9 a.m.–12:30 p.m. Monday–Friday. Dory 9 a.m.–3 p.m. Monday–Friday.* I stood at the bulletin board, wrung pool water from my hair, and tried to guess who was who, while over on the cot Mark—the head guard—played Trivial Pursuit (All Sports Edition) with himself and got a hockey question wrong.

"Okay," I said. "I give up."

"What do you give up?" Mark asked.

"What're my shifts this week?"

He rolled himself off the cot. He smelled of chlorine—we'd both jumped in the pool at the start of our shift to wash away our hangovers—and when he leaned over my shoulder and held a Trivial Pursuit card under a name, the hairs on my neck prickled like they anticipated a drop of sweat might fall from him.

I let my eyes follow the card. *Iago.*

"Oh," I said.

"*Aladdin*, Tamara. The parrot!" He made a squawking noise.

"Yeah, I know."

It turned out that a couple days ago, I'd called the guard shack panicked about a shift I needed to switch ASAP because

I'd forgotten my aunt's birthday dinner. After Britt reassured me that she or Leah could cover the shift, they'd gotten off the phone and into a conversation about what a "spaz" I am. Mark had, naturally, piped up with his best impression of *Aladdin*'s villain, Jafar. So by "Iago" they meant, *Calm yourself, Iago*. This incident apparently prompted Mark to change "Tamara" to "Iago" and then to come up with nicknames for everyone else and change the whole schedule.

"*Mulan* is better than *Aladdin*," I said.

"Psh." He flicked my nose with the Trivial Pursuit card. "You wish you were Mulan."

Mark and I worked at an outdoor pool at a private sports club in the third-wealthiest suburb of Vancouver, one known for attracting a lower calibre of lifeguard than the city pools because a) we were non-union and the pay was shit; b) the pool and its staff only worked three months of the year; and c) the only real requirement for employment besides the NLS certification was being the child of a club member. In three years, the most difficult "save" I had made had been talking a twelve-year-old camper through her first experience with a tampon. Once she came out of the bathroom, she was really embarrassed, so I told her how I had been scared to use tampons for ages because the first time I tried one it got "stuck in the hole." She turned sunstroke-red, and when I followed her gaze and saw Mark in the entrance of the guard shack looking awkward as fuck, I turned sunstroke-red too.

I'd been in love with Mark since I was sixteen. Initially I thought I had a chance with him because he was a little funny-looking, the pinkish sort of white guy who always looked sunburnt, was thick-necked with a weak chin, and had eyes slightly too close to his nose. But it turned out many of the girls who worked at the pool saw the same things in him I did. Over the three years we'd known each other, he had fallen in love and broken up with four different co-workers, wholesome and quiet girl-next-door types who had probably never told a child about that time they'd gotten a tampon stuck in their vagina.

This was the summer of 2016, the first summer Mark had been single since we started working together. I was also single, fresh from a breakup with my freshman fling, who had taken my virginity and given me a new confidence with my body that I was keen to demonstrate. During our shifts together, our hips lightly touching, we joked about Mark's most recent ex—who had cheated on him—and argued over which Disney movie was better: *Aladdin* or *Mulan*. Mark and I both had a bad case of nostalgia, so bad we romanticized not only our own childhoods, but decades of childhoods that had existed before our own. This trait made Mark glow: it drew children and women to him, made him seem like the perfect future father. On rainy days, when no one was in the water, we played Words with Friends and battled for dominance of the Pokémon GO gym that had sprung up over the pool. We'd both hacked the app download before it was available in Canada, so when it was released a week later we were able to recruit all the swim-team kids to our colours. Most of the kids went red with Mark, but some of the more competitive older kids had chosen blue—not to play with me, but to play *against* Mark, who they adored.

I'd thought that maybe he'd finally come around to seeing me the way I saw him. And then he'd gone and nicknamed me Iago, and it felt like the pool deck had fallen out from under me. It was pretty unambiguous: if you secretly want to see someone naked, you don't nickname them after a hyperanxious evil sidekick from a children's movie.

It was a vicious sort of hot summer day, the kind where your swimsuit and hair dry in minutes, and underneath, your blood simmers until you can feel your pulse in your wrists, neck, and knees. Families packed the pool and surrounding picnic area before noon, spraying sunscreen and sharing plates of greasy chicken fingers brought down from the cafeteria above the hockey rink.

Mark and I lounged on the guard chair in our swimsuits, sunglasses, and the communal—and rarely washed—tank tops and ball caps of our official lifeguard uniform. For once, I was thankful for the heat. The sunglasses and frequent jumps in the pool hid the embarrassment and distress I knew circled my eyes. Every few minutes, one of us shouted out a pool rule or asked kids how old they were to make sure no one under the age of eight was swimming without a guardian.

"No running!"

"No swimming under the bulkhead!"

"No noodle fights! I see you, Amy!"

"How old are you?"

"Eight!"

"Yeah, right."

Half the kids in the pool were eight. The junior swim-team kids in particular were notorious "eight-year-olds," because they could actually swim and were encouraged to lie because their parents didn't want to get their hair wet.

"Peter, Ethan, I know you guys aren't eight," Mark said. "Go get one of your parents."

One of the twins took a defiant step off the pool deck and onto the bulkhead.

"Get off the bulkhead, Ethan."

"*You* walk on it."

"I'm a lifeguard, I'm allowed to."

"I'm eight."

"No, you aren't."

"Yeah, well—" and what he said next reeked of rehearsal "—my membership fees pay your salaries and I could get you fired."

"Ethan, my mom's on the board of directors," I said. "We're not going to get fired for doing our job. Go get one of your parents."

He stuck out his tongue at us. "I like the other guard better."

"That's nice."

"The one with bigger boobs."

I must have been sensitive because of the Iago thing because this comment upset me more than I wanted to admit. I was also vaguely annoyed they'd bothered to insult me but left Mark alone. Ethan and Peter both played Pokémon GO on the red team. I was pretty sure neither of them knew my name.

"I don't care. Go get your mom or dad."

Once they were outside the gate, I turned to Mark. "You're sure they're under eight?"

"You know Mimi, at the front desk? She goes to school with their older sister, she told me they just turned six."

"Oh." I wondered what else Mark and Mimi-at-the-front-desk chatted about.

"He must have been talking about Leah," he said. "She's got the biggest tits on staff."

I stood and climbed down from the guard chair, then jumped off the bulkhead and into the pool. When I climbed out, I stretched to highlight how the tank top clung to my C-cups, averting my gaze so I couldn't tell whether Mark noticed or not. It was a stupid, desperate thing to do, and it was hard not to laugh at myself. I remembered being eleven at this pool and trying to swim seductively past the bulkhead because I had a crush on one of the teenage guards. There was something gloriously pathetic about the fact that eight years later I still had the same amount of game. Mark would have found this hilarious if I'd been able to tell him what I was thinking.

As I lowered my arms, I noticed several kids flocking toward the corner of the picnic area nearest the change rooms. "What the hell?"

Mark twisted around in the guard chair and yelled, "What's over there?"

One of the kids shouted back, "There's a Lapras over here!"

"No way!"

In the pool, kids began frantically kicking toward the edge.

"No running," I said. No one listened.

"Fuck," Mark said. We'd both turned around to watch as dozens of adults and children rushed toward the change rooms iPhone-first. "Think there's really a Lapras over there?"

"Probably."

"Watch the pool, Tam."

"Dude."

"I'll grab your phone and catch you one as well, what's your pass code?"

"You better get me one!" I shouted as he jogged across the pool deck. I paused, then added: "No running!" I hoped he'd find the irony funny.

I watched him round the kiddie wading pool and join the pack at the change-room entrances. He held up a phone, and when I saw the bright purple case flash in the sun, my blood went from a simmer to an all-out boil—he'd chosen to catch one for me first. Would he have done that for anyone, I wondered. Blood throbbed where my crossed thighs met. That was the problem with nice guys. You could never tell whether they were treating you specially.

I turned back to the pool and began my left-to-right, top-to-bottom scan. The pool was empty except for a handful of teenagers in the dive tank, a toddler and mom in the shallow end, and three older front crawlers in the far lane.

I stepped down onto the bulkhead, crossed to the other side of the pool, then turned back to scan the blind spots.

A faint stream of red spiralled from under the bulkhead, under the guard chair. When I cranked my head around I could make out a small set of legs and swim trunks.

I jumped into the water before I remembered to blow my whistle.

"Mark!" I screamed.

I blew the whistle and dove.

The shell of the bulkhead fell a foot under the water, but it was enough to conceal someone if they wanted to hide. One of the twins floated face down underneath. I surfaced carefully—the air pocket was only half a foot high—and clamped my hands over his jaw and the back of his head the way we were taught to when we suspected a head or spinal injury. I rolled him so he was face up under the bulkhead. I was surprised to see Peter's face—I'd expected Ethan. Strands of blood mixed with his black hair leaked between my fingers. It was too dark to tell whether he was breathing.

I'd only ever done this with classmates and co-workers.

Mark surfaced across from me.

"Fuck," he said. "We need to get him out."

"I don't know if he's breathing."

Mark swam over, gave two breaths, and pressed two fingers against Peter's neck. "He's got a pulse. We'll have to take him under."

"How?"

"Stay calm, Tamara. You can do this. On my count, roll him back onto his front and kick down. I'll meet you on the other side." He leaned over and gave two more breaths. "One, two, three, *roll*."

I pulled Peter under the water.

Once we were back in the lane pool, I rolled Peter onto his front and began to kick over toward the shallow end. Mark was in the water with the spinal board, waiting.

My head tingled as a hundred eyes landed on us. I heard a woman shout that the ambulance was coming.

Ten hours later, Mark and I sat across from each other at the Lion's Head and ironically cheersed the last glasses of our third pitcher to capturing a Lapras. Mark had given his number to one of the paramedics, but no one had gotten in touch to let us know whether Peter would be okay. He had woken up and begun to cry as we loaded him onto the spinal board, which we took as a good sign. My mother had texted me earlier to say the board had been notified that we'd been distracted during the accident, and that Mark had been outside the pool area. *I'm sorry, honey,* she wrote. *They're going to do an investigation.* I wrote that I didn't know what that meant. She said we'd talk when I got home.

"The brats," Mark said. "You know they waited until we weren't looking to sneak in, and hid under the bulkhead." Ethan had climbed out of the pool with the rest of the kids, and hadn't noticed Peter wasn't with him. We figured he'd been heading out to grab his iPhone too but had miscalculated when he surfaced and hit his head.

"You did a great job," he said.

"Thanks," I said, even though I didn't believe him. "You too."

"Cheers!" he said again. "To your first rescue."

"We don't know for sure it's a rescue yet." The beer flooded my eyes and I raised my glass and awkwardly clinked his.

"Tamara." He downed a third of the glass. "Tamara, I'm sure he's fine."

I didn't say anything.

"Tam, jam, thank you, ma'am."

"Bam."

"What?"

"It's wham, bam, thank you, ma'am. I think."

"That's what I said."

"Oh."

"Tamara." His voice was liquid. "We gotta change your name."

"I like Tamara."

"You're at least a Princess Jasmine."

Despite everything, I smiled. "How's that any better than Iago?" I said, even though I knew it *was* better. "She doesn't do anything. She doesn't save anyone."

He pointed a finger at me. "You... are right." He poked my nose. "What then? You want to be Elsa, like all the kids?"

"Fuck *Frozen*. You know who I want to be."

"Mulan."

I nodded.

"You know what?" He slapped the table. "I've never actually seen it."

"Are you shitting me? We've argued all summer over which movie is better and you've never even seen it?"

"We could fix that now."

We paid our tab, left our cars at the bar, and walked up to his place. We entered the basement via the backyard, through French doors, quietly so we didn't wake his parents. I'd never been in Mark's house before. The carpet and sofa were expensive enough to be classy, but old enough to be comfortable. A large television hung from the wall across the couch. Mark turned it on and stumbled through menu options until he figured out how to rent *Mulan* on iTunes. He wavered and I realized that, as drunk as I was, Mark was further gone. He'd probably matched my drinks three to one.

We got a text message from my mother halfway through the second song. *Just heard. They're keeping him overnight, but he'll be fine. Concussion. Not sure if any effects from lack of oxygen.* And then: *When will you be home?*

I texted back. *Thanks for letting me know. Be home late, don't wait up.*

Are you OK?

Not really, but yes.

Love you, sweetie.

Thanks mom, love you too.

Mark nudged me. "See? You're a hero."

"Heroine."

"Don't be sexist."

"*Heroine*'s a funny word. The gender switches like four times within it. *He, her, hero, heroine.*"

"What about heroin?" Mark said it slowly, enunciating every syllable.

I nudged him back. "Heroin doesn't have a gender."

On the screen, Mulan tried and failed to impress Li Shang, the army captain who was training her and the other misfit recruits. At the end of the movie, she won both the war and his heart. *Is that all it takes?* I thought. It was the first movie my parents had bought me. I knew every line.

Mark nudged me and I nudged him and then we were wrestling and then he had me pinned on the couch. Our faces hovered centimetres from each other. I'd imagined this moment for years. His eyes drooped. He couldn't focus to meet my gaze.

I could feel my heartbeat everywhere.

I wanted to tell him I loved him. Instead I said, "This isn't appropriate."

"What?" He jumped up so quickly he almost fell off the couch.

"You're my boss."

"I'm drunk."

"Yes," I said. "That too."

I got up and walked over to the doors. I opened one, then turned back. "When we're both sober—" I started to say, but his face was in his hands.

"What about Mimi?" he said.

"Mimi?"

"From the front desk."

"Right." I stepped outside and closed the door behind me.

It was a thirty-minute walk home, straight uphill. I was drunk as fuck, and when I got home I snuck into my parents' liquor cabinet, poured myself a glass of Crown Royal, and got even drunker. I was nineteen, I told myself. Nineteen and stupid. It was okay to be nineteen and stupid with a broken heart. It doesn't matter.

The moonlight caught car windows and reflected my face back at me. I watched myself climb the hill and promised myself I would remember this for the rest of my life.

THUNDERSTRUCK

Head. Game. Four minutes left in the third, o-o. My stomach lurches and sends bile up my esophagus and into the back of my mouth. I swallow. Puck drops. I'm too slow and lose—on the bench, someone says *shit*. I fly up to intercept a pass from their defence, but I forget to watch the winger and she crushes me against the boards, chips the puck back to the D as she dekes around us. Skate it off. I feel delirious. Head-in-the-game. The puck's in our end. They shoot wide and Vanessa sends it off the boards to Juliet. I wheel to skate with her. Their defender is caught in our zone, two-on-one, the remaining D goes for Juliet as she skates across the blue line, but she sends it back to me. I slap low, aim for the five-hole—but something hard hits me from behind and I fly forward, land shoulder-hip, and slide backwards into the boards. Another jet of bile fills my mouth, and I can't swallow. The whistle blows. I push myself up with my gloves and skate to the bench. Juliet's next to me. "You okay?"

I nod and step off the ice. There's a garbage can on the side of the bench. I pull off my helmet, drop my gloves, yank the lid off the can, and lean over the bench and vomit orange ribbons of water, Gatorade, and partially digested bread.

This is the moment when it occurs to me that I'm pregnant.

I can hear our head coach, Luke, shouting at the ref. "Two minutes? That was cross-checking, she should be out of here!" Then: "Rossi. Did you hit your head?"

I'd had an upset stomach all week—I'd thought nerves, but since when did I get nerves over a stupid tournament? No period—not that I have much in the way of periods anyway, nothing worth buying tampons for. No period for—how long?—two, three months? Not abnormal, but not good—and the puking and nausea are definitely not normal, and everyone knows condoms aren't one hundred per cent effective, and oh my fucking god, I am so stupid and I am so pregnant.

Bile burns its way up my throat. I cough and spit. I blink and phosphenes hover over discarded candy wrappers, power-drink containers, fruit peels and cores, like portals to other dimensions, tears in the fabric of space-time that hover just out of reach. I consider diving in headfirst. "I'm fine," I say.

"Chang, ask for a time out! Time out, ref!"

My vision clears and I look up. In the bleachers, two men with clipboards take notes. From that angle, they would have seen that I didn't hit my head. There's no way they could know, I remind myself.

They just think you're weak.

"Rossi!"

"I'm fine!" I pick my helmet up off the bench and put it on, then grab my gloves from the ground. "I can go back out."

Luke puts a hand on either side of my head; his fingers brush loose hair from my ponytail, sending shivers like spiders crawling over my scalp and down my spine. He leans in close and stares into my eyes. I blink and jerk my head back, but I'm trapped in my helmet.

"Bench, Rossi. Biel, Naps—you too. Malik, Johnson, Lim—get out there. D stay on." Shaz, Tasha, and Amy jump the boards onto the ice. "Three minutes left, people." Juliet steps through the door. Her face twists in anger as she takes the bench next to me. Luke's nickname for her—Naps—is a play on both her last name, Napier, and Napoleon, a not-so-subtle dig at her delicate five-foot-three frame. I think Luke meant it as a compliment, but Juliet has told me that all she hears when he says it is *you are too small for hockey*. Secretly, she reminds me of an elf. Blond and tiny, except for her eyes and ears.

Luke leans over the bench. "What do we want?" he shouts.

"To win!" we shout.

"So what do we have to do?"

"BRING THE THUNDER!"

Sticks bash against ice and boards and dull Mississauga's chants from their bench. The whistle blows.

Juliet passes me my water bottle. "You sure you're okay?" she asks.

I nod. I unclip my mask and drink deeply, washing the acidic aftertaste from the back of my throat. "She didn't hit me that hard."

Luke glances back at us. "Rossi, you think you can go out?"

"Yes, sir!"

I join him at the gate just as Vanessa takes a slapshot from the point, through five players, over the goalie's shoulder, top-left net. The whistle blows, one-nothing. Our bench erupts in cheers. I swallow another mouthful of bile. It should have been me. I swallow the thought.

Outside the rink, I load my gear and board the rental bus, taking my seat near the front beside Vanessa. I want to hide in the back, press my fingers against my abs, and search for a heartbeat. (Although: would there be a heartbeat yet? And if so, could I feel it beneath the layers of muscle? Could a child even grow in there, or would it be crushed by my six-pack?) (I hope so.) I wish I'd paid better attention in health class. My hands itch to reach for my phone so I can google these and so many other questions. But I can't risk anyone seeing me.

Luke kneels on his seat and addresses the team, arms slung casually over his backrest, as Rosa, his assistant coach, leans on the gas and tears out of the parking lot. "Way to bring the thunder, ladies!" he shouts. "We're still in this!"

We drum our hands on the seats in front of us, chanting the opening word of AC/DC's "Thunderstruck." *Thunder! Thunder! Thunder! Thunder!* This is my third year on the Greater Vancouver Midget AAA Thunder. I've done this so many times, it's a reflex.

Vanessa sits up and turns to face the team. The embroidered A on her blue-and-gold track jacket matches the C on mine. I'm too slow. She elbows me in the ribs, and I clamber up beside her. My eyes sting; I hope the glint is mistaken for passion, or excitement. I smile too widely.

Vanessa's creative. She adapts pop songs into team chants for all of our away games and tournaments. *Gotta keep it fresh,* she said, as she handed out Duo-Tangs of lyrics for us to memorize on the four-hour flight from Vancouver to Toronto.

She elbows me again—she's already singing.

I channel my inner Taylor Swift.

'Cause the winners gonna win, win, win, win, win
And the losers gonna lose, lose, lose, lose, lose
We're just gonna bruise, bruise, bruise, bruise, bruise
Bruise you all! Bruise you all!
And skaters gonna skate, skate, skate, skate, skate
If you make a mistake, take, take, take, take
Baby, we're just gonna break, break, break, break, break
Breakaway! Breakaway! Score!

At least two teammates shout "break your legs" instead of "breakaway," and "whore" instead of "score." At the back of the bus, I can see our goalie, Karen, grinning. I glance sideways at Vanessa; her jaw clenches as she sings. She'll tell anyone who will listen that she's a feminist, and hates when the other girls use "sexist" slurs. Plus she spends hours on these songs.

I wonder whether I can call myself a feminist, when I hold my tongue on the ice (most of the time), but I can't stop thinking all the sexist slurs. What's a word for a woman that ends with U-N-T? Aunt. Yeah, not that one. I laugh to myself, and immediately feel bad about it.

The truth is, the chants and songs are all tradition and bravado; we're David screaming at Goliath, the protagonists in the first half of every sports movie ever. Luke may be ex-NHL and have the jaw of a Disney prince, but he's no Mr. Miyagi. (Hell, he never left the fourth line in a five-year career, and everyone knows fourth-liners are the bookmarks of hockey games.) BC teams don't stand a chance against powerhouses from Alberta, Ontario, and Quebec. To put it in perspective, Mississauga is a middle-of-the-pack Ontario team, and we're the provincial champs. Even with Karen in net, we won't survive the round robin—we've already lost two games and need to win three of the next four to even have a chance at semifinals. We're here so our better players can be seen by scouts from the east coast universities, junior hockey clubs, and the National Women's Development Team. Weeks ago, as Luke ran his hands down my rock-hard, fetus-crushing abs, over my hipbone, and between my legs, he whispered that the scouts had two names at the top of their list of girls to watch.

"Phillips," I said, meaning Karen, "and?"

"And," he said.

I gasped as he pressed his fingers into me.

"And you, Rossi," he said. We've been sleeping together since the start of the season, but he still calls me by my last name.

"And me," I repeated.

There's an expression: talent, hard work, and luck—you need at least two to succeed. I think only an idiot relies on luck.

I'm seventeen. He's nearly forty, my coach, my trainer, my nutritionist, my mentor, my boss, my best chance at what passes for a professional career in women's hockey. I wonder whether I can call myself a feminist when I'm so willing to be a victim.

We have an hour to shower, stretch, and relax before dinner. I ditch my roommates after my shower, but the hotel shop doesn't have pregnancy tests. I vomit again in the lobby bathroom before meeting the team to walk to the Old Spaghetti Factory (rules include: tomato-based sauces and lean meats only, no pop, no dessert). I struggle to choke down my penne.

"Are you okay?" Juliet touches my arm. "You're not eating."

"I had a granola bar at the hotel," I say.

Across from us, Shaz laughs. "So what? So did I." Her plate is empty. We normally eat between three and four thousand calories per day.

At the end of the table, I can see Luke watching me and Shaz talk. I get up to go to the bathroom. Juliet follows me.

"What's going on, Jill?"

There's no point lying—with the exception of the two years before this one, we've played together since we were four. The two years I'd played AAA without her, before she made the team, had created a distance between us I can't quite put words to, but even if Juliet no longer knows every kink in my back and every knot in my soul, she still knows my scent so well she could walk blindfolded to my hockey bag in a crowded change room. I kick open all the stall doors before I answer. "I think I'm pregnant."

"What the actual fuck?"

"Shut up!"

"What do you mean," she says, quieter this time, "you think you're pregnant?"

"I'm nauseous, I'm late—"

"You're probably overtraining—"

"My breasts are tender," I hiss.

Juliet's eyes dip down. "Do you even have breasts anymore? I thought you exercised those into pectorals."

"That's not science."

"But I mean, they could be sore from overtraining. Have you even had sex?"

"Of course I've had sex," I snap. "Why would I think I'm pregnant if I hadn't had sex?"

"I don't know! Who the hell did you have sex with anyway? You don't go to parties, you have no free time, and as far as I know, you don't have a boyfriend. So cut me a fucking break, okay, I'm processing." She pauses. "But you haven't taken a test yet?"

"No."

"Okay, so that's the first thing."

"So where the fuck do we get one of those?"

She's already on her phone. "There's a pharmacy about a fifteen-minute walk from the hotel. We have seventy-five minutes between breakfast and our first game tomorrow. We can go then."

"Right."

She puts her phone back in the pocket of her track pants. "So who was it?"

"What?"

"Duh, Jill. Sperm-boy."

"Oh," I say. "No one you know."

When I was little, my father told me never to say you're going to do something, just do it. If you tell people about your dreams, it's like you expect others to make them happen for you. You'll take credit for accomplishments before they are accomplished. You won't work as hard.

I think there's a second reason—if you keep your dreams to yourself, then your failures will go unnoticed.

Even though I listened to my father's advice and never said it out loud—not to him or my mom, or Luke, not even to Juliet despite the fact that she knew and I knew she knew and she knew I knew she knew but didn't want to admit it— for as long as I can remember, my goal has been to play on the Canadian Olympic Women's Hockey Team. Deeper still, I dreamed of playing in the NHL. This was a desire so deep I kept it from myself until early last summer, when the invitation to the U18 National Team training camp I'd been waiting for—but not expecting, winners never expect—didn't come. Only two girls from BC got the phone call: a burly forward from the Okanagan, and Karen.

When Karen called to tell me the news, I pressed my phone against my ear so hard I hung up on her. If at first you don't succeed, don't cry about it.

I grabbed my gear and car keys, and drove to the nearest rink for drop-in stick-and-puck. The best thing to do, I knew, was to outskate my broken heart.

It was the kind of beautiful, hot summer day that drives even the most dedicated hockey enthusiasts outside. The ice was soft to step on, and I could feel perspiration pool between my skin and pads before I'd taken three strides. Four guys a few years older than me scrimmaged at one end. At the other, Luke, wearing only track pants and a T-shirt, was taking shots at a small but quick goalie. I recognized her jersey from tryouts.

He called out as I stepped on the ice. "Rossi! Great timing! Get your ass over here!"

The goalie skated over as I joined him.

Luke jerked his head at her. "You remember Andrea, new goalie for the Thunder? Ono, Jillian Rossi, she'll be your captain."

"Replacing Karen?" I said stupidly.

"You got heatstroke, Rossi? Replacing Stevens. Phillips is still starting."

Andrea held out a glove and I shook it.

"Nice to officially meet you," she said.

"You're in luck, Ono. Rossi here shoots like a sniper."

"Oh, I know. I was terrified when I saw her coming."

"Thanks," I said.

I was less like a sniper than a pitching machine. After a few minutes, the heat overwhelmed me and I skated back to the bench and pulled off my helmet, jersey, shoulder pads, and elbow pads.

I've thought about this a lot in the last few months: I had intended to pull my jersey back on when I went to take my gear off, but then I left it crumpled on the bench and skated back over to Luke and Andrea in my sports bra. Superficially, I justified the decision because of the heat, the struggling rink air conditioner, but even at the time I was aware that I'd straightened my posture slightly more than natural, that I deliberately twisted my body so my ribs and abdominal muscles rippled from my armpits to my hockey pants, and from my chest up to my chin, like a penny had been dropped into the notch where my clavicles met. It's not that I wanted the five men on the ice to find me attractive—not entirely. I wanted them to see that I was *strong*. I wanted them to both want me and to be intimidated by me. I wanted them to want to prove their own strength against mine. I was too tall, too muscular, too lacking in traditional feminine curves—but I'd imagined that Luke's hands lingered on my neck when he rubbed out shoulder knots between games, and it always left me with an adrenaline high that somehow made me feel powerful, or maybe beautiful.

For an hour and a half Luke and I took turns firing rounds of pucks at Andrea, who skillfully stopped all but a few. I couldn't tell for sure, but I thought she looked smug beneath her mask.

I took a long time in the shower so I was surprised to see Luke still hanging around when I came out of the change room.

"Hey, Rossi," he said. "I'm sorry to hear about the camp. The fuckers don't know what they're missing."

I opened my mouth to say I didn't care, but instead I said, "So much for the Olympics." My voice sounded so small, like it had been squeezed through a long straw.

He clamped his hands on my shoulders so tightly I thought I would bruise. I could smell mint Tic Tacs on his breath. "Rossi, listen to me. If you work hard, you can be good enough for the Olympic team. You *are* good enough. I know for a fact that you were considered for that camp. The girls they picked are on stronger teams, they play with better players, who make them look better than they are."

I realized I was crying.

"Rossi, you listening? They made a mistake."

I nodded.

He asked if I was okay to drive and offered me a ride home, and I said no and accepted, aware on some level that neither his offer nor my answer really made sense.

We stopped off at his house to pick up something or other. That was the first time.

Puck drops. I send it back to Evie, who passes to Vanessa, who takes off toward the offensive zone. I scream for the pass, but she sends it across the ice to Marion instead. Intercepted by their centre. She catches me flat-footed and zips past the blue line into our zone.

Earlier that morning, I sat on the toilet seat of a Starbucks bathroom with three positive pregnancy tests between the fingers of one hand, like Wolverine's claws. I trailed them across the stall wall as I shook the fourth test dry. The little crosses are the same colour as the blue line.

"Rossi! Skate!"

I realize I'm staring at the blue line.

Panic grips my heart and heats into anger. Vanessa's out of position, it's three-on-one. It's already one-nothing for them. I can't let them score. I can't be on the ice when they score.

Head-in-the-game.

I fly, but I can't outskate the burning in my lungs, in my legs. My stomach grumbles. I'd opted to play with it empty, and two periods in I regret my decision.

When was my last period?

Head-in-the-game, Rossi.

You may resume normal emotions after the fucking game.

I'm catching her. I lean my shoulder into hers, stretch my stick for the puck, but she fakes a shot and passes to the winger, who one-times it to the top corner. I'm too late, too slow.

How accurate are they? I'd asked.

Juliet leaned against the stall door, holding my boxes. She peered at a small piece of paper. *Ninety-seven per cent.*

Help me out here, you're good at math. Three times three times three times three per cent.

It's a beautiful shot. One in a million.

I'm sorry.

Karen's glove pops out of nowhere, like a monster in a horror film, and bats the puck out of the air. She falls forward on it as the winger swings to hit it again, and Vanessa arrives just in time to slide in front of her and block her stick before it hits Karen in the head. The player slashes Vanessa trying to get at the net, and Vanessa shoves her back as the ref blows the whistle.

Karen rolls over to a sitting position. She shakes off her blocker and grabs her glove arm above the elbow with her bare hand. She jerks her arm up with a grunt and pops her shoulder back into place. Behind her, in the bleachers, a man types something on an iPad.

What are you going to do?

What do you mean?

Juliet searched for the numbers of clinics and added them to my phone. *Do you need help calling? What are you going to tell Luke?*

I stopped running the pregnancy tests along the stall wall just before I whacked the toilet paper dispenser. *Why the fuck would I need to tell him anything?*

I don't think you're allowed to play if you're pregnant.

Fuck off, Jules. I'm not telling Luke, and I'm not missing any games. What's the worst that can happen? Someone knocks me in the gut and I save a few hundred dollars?

I swallow a mouthful of bile.

"What, Rossi, you gonna be sick?" Karen says. She wags her arm at me. "Man up, it's just a dislocated shoulder."

"Woman up," Vanessa says.

"How about shut up."

The whistle blows.

Later that night, I slip out of our hotel room after everyone is asleep. I close the door in time with Juliet's snoring. I take the stairs two floors up.

When Luke opens his door, I realize I'm going to sleep with him. To not go through with it would require a conversation I'm not ready—I will never be ready—to have. I let him pull me into the room, I let him peel off my shirt and my sports bra. I let him dig his fingers deep into my back, to knead out the muscle knots, then to slide his hands over my shoulders to my breasts. I let him. I let him. I let him. It all feels good on the surface. I try to focus on that instead of the guilt. It's not like I can get pregnant again, I remind myself. It will all be over soon. I squeeze my eyes shut until the lids light up, I send my mind through the phosphene portals, far away from my body, and separate the part of me that screams for more from the part of me that screams for him to stop.

I'm not an idiot: even after the first time, when he traced his fingers around the perimeter of a bruise on my thigh I'd gotten from a slapshot, I never thought we'd fall in love.

It was never about that.

My stomach lurches as he pushes deeper toward my bladder. *I spoke to a US college scout today.* His voice is so far away. *I told them you were one of the best players I'd seen in a long time.*

I believe him because, for a while at least, it drowns out the litany of failures that scroll through my head. No scholarship offers yet. No invite to the training camp. Never made it to the Midget AAA Nationals (knocked out of the Pacific Region qualifiers by Edmonton last year, and the Fraser Valley two years ago). Then the smaller failures: I haven't scored a goal yet this tournament. I wasn't even on the ice for yesterday's game-winner. I let myself get pregnant. I let him get me pregnant.

You're good enough, Rossi. You just gotta focus, gotta work, gotta give everything to the game.

I arch my back. Focus.

PIECES

HAIR

He won't stop touching your hair. You've asked him not to before, because it makes you feel uncomfortable or perhaps because it makes you uncomfortable that it doesn't make you feel more uncomfortable, or perhaps just because you're supposed to say it makes you feel uncomfortable. (You are unsure.) Now you can't bring yourself to say it again. He's wrapped your hair around his fingers like infants swaddled in blankets. You have the sense that if you break the connection before he's ready, he'll come unglued and collapse in pieces at your feet. You wonder whether this sense comes from perception or from a secret, dark part of you that likes to think of yourself as a person who has great meaning to others. You want to recoil but at the same time you want to press your forehead into his palm because maybe it would be easier. By the time he withdraws his hand and tells you he'll see you around, you're exhausted and you hate yourself. You promise to come back for the rest of your things in a week. Ten days later, you're one step out the door with the last box and you finally tell him you don't think you can be friends. He turns up the heat on the stove, and the water in his pot begins to boil. You let the door swing shut behind you.

EYES

Your eyes are so deep-set in your head you can't use an eyelash curler. This is something you romanticize about yourself, even though it is not particularly romantic and could probably be solved by buying a smaller eyelash curler. You once smoked too much weed and looked in a mirror and convinced yourself that tears flatter your eyes because they saturate the grey until it appears blue. Your friends inform you, repeatedly, that you are not in fact an attractive crier, but that's okay, no one is.

EARS

One time in elementary school, kids took turns making louder and louder noises to try to get you to look up from your book. When the winner slammed his palm against your desk and you jumped, a half-dozen kids laughed and said they'd been trying to wake you for nearly five minutes. Over fifteen years later, you still have the ability to tune out the world completely. You have been criticized for not listening, for ignoring problems in your reality and hoping that by ignoring them they will somehow disappear. You play important conversations over and over in your head before you have them, and then are surprised when people go off-script. You think you understand people but you always get their dialogue wrong. In the weeks after the breakup, before you move out, you listen closely to the rare words he lets fall like confetti when you cross paths. Even when you catch every syllable, you aren't sure what significance to affix to his sentences. You're overthinking; you're taking words too literally. He tells you that just because he talks about an idea, it doesn't mean he'll act on it. He says he doesn't always mean what he says, and you wonder if he means that.

MOUTH

You're the worst liar in the world. Of all your pieces, your mouth is the most likely to betray you. You have a nervous cough that only appears when you feel an urgency to be quiet: as the lights go down in a playhouse, during moments of silence, in the long hours it took you to fall asleep next to him every night before you left. Like that cough, you are able to hold secrets in your chest only until the stakes get too high. Then your lungs begin to itch and it all comes out.

LUNGS

You have a very mild form of asthma that is triggered only by extreme exercise and extreme emotions. You got the blue puffer at fifteen after you collapsed on the ice because your hockey team lost a playoff game. (You're too competitive. This is something he tells you a lot. You care too much. You should stop caring. You will wear yourself out.) Over a decade later, you discover your lungs can fail you even when you try to hold yourself as still as possible.

HEART

You think you have a pain in your heart. It's been two months since the breakup, five weeks since you moved, and you're out with someone new. When you describe the sensation to your date and place a fist between your breasts, he assures you the pain is too high to be in your heart. It's probably muscular, he says. You probably pulled something during hockey. Besides, you can't *feel* your heart. He asks you for a metaphor. You tell him it's like there's a balloon in your chest pushing up against your sternum, trying to break free. This isn't quite right, but it's the best you can do.

LIVER
The other pieces blame your liver for metabolizing the relationship for as long as it did. Three weeks before the breakup, he's out of town visiting family and you get five beers deep and admit to a friend that the last four days of your life might technically count as—you air-quote—a "bender," in that you have spent every hour stoned, drunk, or asleep. You have a Tupperware full of marijuana you got from your brother, and you are spending your nights butting joint after joint out on the glass ashtray, watching Hollywood movies about men who are dumped and siding with the ex-girlfriends, plugging away at the most mindless parts of your freelance web and communications work while neglecting all tasks that require a working brain cell. When your friend asks you what's wrong, your lungs begin to itch and your mouth tells her everything.

HANDS
You are a hand talker. You enunciate each letter with twists of your wrists. After each statement, you clarify, and then you clarify the clarification, and then you clarify the clarification of the clarification (et cetera), and your hands build momen-

tum as you grow more and more drunk and more and more distressed. The problem, you tell your friend, hands waving, is that the facts make it sound worse than it is. You tell her you feel like you've been pouring your love into a cracked cup. You hold your hands out, palms up, and spread your fingers to demonstrate. She stills your hands by placing hers on your wrists. She says you are not his caretaker. She says she understands.

LEGS

The day after the breakup, you come home to find him drunk. He puts his hand in your hair and tells you he doesn't deserve to live. You start to cry, and you beg him to call his mother, his sister, his other sister, his best friend, his other best friend. He says he doesn't want to. Your legs collapse from under you and now you're sitting on the floor. You pull your cellphone out. You ask him who you can call. He says no one. You tell him he has to pick someone. He says he doesn't want anyone else there. You want to leave but you can't leave him alone. You realize that after two and a half years the only number you have is his sister's and she lives on the other side of the country. He dumps the bookshelves in the spare bedroom, which you've been using as an office. He tells you it's okay, you can stay roommates. He looked up beds online, and they aren't that expensive, you can buy another bed. You say the couch is fine. He drags the shelves into the living room and then starts to take apart your ratty IKEA sofa. You text your brother, *please come over*. When your brother arrives, he hugs you and then crosses the living room to assist with the furniture. You feel stupid standing there and watching the two men tear apart and reassemble your apartment, so you help. You start to lift one section of the couch. Your brother gently reminds you to lift with your legs.

SKIN

In ninth grade, a group of boys from your school creates their perfect woman from pieces of you and your female classmates, one body part per girl. They read the list out at a house party. Each girl nods her head as her best feature is named and added. (The girl they take the lips from smiles, like a reflex.) You patiently wait to hear which piece they'll take from you, even though the whole exercise is disturbing and you know you're all "being objectified." The thing is, you're curious, you want to know what they'll say about you, and so you sit and nod with the rest of the girls until the boys get to your name and say *skin*. *Skin*. You don't know how to respond. You had prepared yourself to be reduced to a part, but your skin? You imagine them peeling you into a single strip and wrapping it around the pieces taken from the other girls. You feel hurt, but you try to hide your discomfort because no one else seems upset. After a few minutes and two more pieces, you excuse yourself and sit in the bathroom until you're okay to return to the party. Years later, four months before you leave, he makes an off-the-cuff remark that it *feels like a burden to touch you*, and you roll up a sweater sleeve and you think about that party. You trail a finger along your own arm. You think: your skin is so soft, but so thin.

BONES

You never understood the phrase *bone-weary* until you told him it was over. The day after he and your brother moved the couch into the spare bedroom, he dumps all your clothes at the foot. He tells you you can stay there for as long as you need to, but your ears hear *you can stay here as long as I need you to*. You sign a new lease in secret and break the news to him a week later. You can't sleep. You can't focus. A few days before you move out, a migraine splits you in two and you come home early to an empty apartment. You pop two Advil and walk to the bedroom and crawl into your old bed with your clothes on. Once you're down you can't get up. Your bones are tired. It feels like they have been filled with lead. The comforter is yellow and orange, and for a brief, romantic moment you think of yourself as a fly slowly becoming trapped in amber. The walls and ceiling blur, like the world is a watercolour painting and someone has tipped a glass over onto it. Your eyes wash away at the periphery. In the seconds before you slip into rest, you promise yourself that this is the last time you'll ever be this weak.

ANYTHING TO MAKE YOU HAPPY

Lisa had promised herself she would leave if Jamie didn't start taking the pills. She rationalized that it was probably easier to put back together a heart that's been broken all at once than to try to reconstruct one that's been chipped away over a longer period of time, eroded into sand.

Sometimes Lisa wondered what happened to all the little pieces of broken heart. At first she thought they might poison your bloodstream, and that was why it was impossible to stay in a situation where your heart breaks just a little every day. Fragments of heart might even end up in your brain, where they could destroy your dopamine and serotonin pathways until you literally forgot how to be happy. (She liked the last part of this theory until she realized that in this very specific case, she was metaphorically implying that Jamie's depression was contagious, which seemed super-stigmatizing and counterproductive and possibly even ableist.) Then Lisa figured the broken-heart sand probably ended up in your digestive system, which was why some people got the anxiety shits. This was the theory she liked best.

She had originally decided to give him at least four months, six at the most, but after her trip to the clinic that morning, everything had become more urgent.

She wasn't heartless, she reminded herself as she picked up the bottle of 5-HTP and examined it for evidence of missing tablets. The ultimatum was not *get better or I am gone*. She just wanted him to *try*. The cocktail of over-the-counter supplements had been a compromise anyway. She wasn't even harping on him anymore to go see a therapist, or to go see a doctor for a prescription for antidepressants. She just wanted him to be happy. *Them* to be happy, she silently corrected herself and then her throat constricted.

The tears lasted only two or three minutes this time—three anxiety-inducing minutes where she both feared and prayed Jamie would open their bedroom door and wander out in his boxer shorts and catch her hunched over the sink, hyperventilating and sobbing.

Be stronger. She focused on her breath. *You don't have to be this person.*

You are in control.

The fits had been happening more and more frequently, but she could still stop them as long as no one caught her crying and asked her what was wrong. Then she would lose it. It wasn't their fault. People just wanted to help. It was something in her biology, some sort of deficiency or chronic attention-seeking that made it impossible for her to calm down. As long as she was alone, she could tell herself her tears were authentic, not just for show. After all, you can't be performative without an audience.

Lisa didn't have depression, not like what Jamie had. She had tons of energy and an all-too-intact sex drive, and for the most part considered herself an optimistic person. Just an optimistic person who was unusually bad at dealing with stressful situations.

This time, however, a part of Lisa wanted Jamie to catch her in the middle of the fit and ask her what was wrong so she'd be forced to tell him she was pregnant. She didn't know how she'd get the nerve up otherwise. After living together for three years, she probably knew Jamie better than anyone else, but she'd never been able to get a clear answer out of him as to whether he wanted children—sometimes he talked about having a family of at least three kids, other times he'd say that bringing a child into this fucked-up world was the most selfish thing a person could do, and once he'd said he was worried Lisa was too anxious to make a good mother—and she didn't know how he'd react to a surprise pregnancy, especially when on the rare times they still had sex Jamie would check that she was still on the birth control pill.

She *was* on the pill, but had gotten careless about it because Jamie's sex drive was so low they'd gone nearly three months without even kissing on the mouth. *Please come cuddle me.* It had become a daily request, and he always obliged and came and lay down next to her and wrapped his arms around her for a few minutes, but five weeks ago Lisa had broken down and confronted him.

He got very quiet and awkward when she suggested his low libido had to do with his depression, and asked her if it had ever occurred to her that he was just asexual? She'd said that if that was true it meant he didn't love her, and he'd said he did love her, more than anything, *please stop crying, moo, what about companionate love?* He said the whole idea that couples had to have sex all the time or there was something wrong with the relationship was just a myth perpetuated by Hollywood and other mainstream media. *It's just cultural pressure,* he said. *You should know better than to fall for that stuff. In Japan, the culture's different. People almost never have sex.*

I don't think that's true.

No, it is, they call them herbivore men.

Bullshit. And then, in a small voice even she recognized as pathetic, *you're not even Japanese.* But then she googled it later and found an article about herbivore men on Wikipedia. The expression made her uncomfortable, as it seemed to imply that heterosexual sex was equivalent to some sort of violent act where the man consumes the woman.

Lisa couldn't accept this idea. She wanted to believe in love.

A few days after the conversation about herbivore men, Jamie had come home from the university and wrapped his arms around her, kissed up and down her neck, and carried her into the bedroom. She didn't want to wreck the moment, awkward and stilted as it already was, so she didn't tell him she'd been late taking a couple of her birth control pills that week. She told herself it was unlikely to matter; the risk was so low. The next day, she'd bought him all the supplements and begged him to take them, trying to subtly convey her ultimatum without ever actually saying, *I'm leaving you if you don't try to get better.*

She screwed the lid back on the bottle. *Why are you so fucking stupid?* she asked herself.

She replaced the 5-HTP on the shelf next to the sink, between the vitamin D and the vitamin B complex. It had been over a month since she had bought the bottles on the recommendation of Claire, one of the visual arts instructors at her work, who claimed to have "all the mental healths" (her words) and swore these "natural remedies" saved her life. If Jamie had been following Claire's instructions, at least sixty pills—one-third of the bottle—would be gone. Instead it was almost full.

Be tougher. She picked at the skin under her nail of her right index finger, until blood began to pool, then pressed her finger into the counter. She breathed into the pain as it shivered through her hand and up her arm.

She'd promised herself she would leave if he didn't start to try.

She'd also never said that promise out loud.

Lisa was excellent at swallowing her thoughts before the words could touch her tongue. Thoughts only had power if you made them material by saying them out loud. Verbalization was commitment. Verbalization created truths. This was how people curated their lives.

She believed that as long as you didn't say a thought out loud, eventually, with patience, there was a chance you could make it go away. She had made a lot of negative thoughts disappear this way, but she couldn't get rid of this one: *I am not happy.*

This was what she was thinking, over and over, as she lay supine on the gallery floor the following Monday and stared up at the LED lights, her stomach roiling with morning sickness. *I am not happy.* No. Worse than that: *I am unhappy.*

She told herself she didn't give a fuck if Greg, the visual arts manager, came in and found her in the middle of "his" gallery, not today. She used to come in the gallery all the time to unwind back before he was hired, but she wasn't as comfortable around him as she had been around Ainsley, his predecessor. *Who gives a fuck if he thinks you're crazy?* But then she listened for the sound of his office door opening because she knew this was a lie.

How did a mother's moods affect a fetus? she wondered. What happens when you grow a child with a genetic predisposition to sadness in a body stressed with it? The clock was ticking. She was five and a half weeks pregnant. She had ten more to make up her mind. Would a child destroy Jamie, or would she—Lisa had taken to thinking of the growing clump of cells in her uterus as a girl—finally give him—give *them*—something to live for?

When Lisa and Jamie first started dating, she'd thought that if she was good enough, she could make him happy. Jamie had revealed his long history with depression to her through an anecdote on their eleventh date: how, before he started at the university, he'd taken a job at a small environmental non-profit thinking he could help save the world, only to realize the whole thing was essentially a scam to get government funding for the for-profit tech company owned by the executive director. After a day spent writing a grant application to produce an educational app Jamie knew no one would ever use, he'd broken down on public transit. *I started laughing*, he said, *and I couldn't stop.*

Lisa sat on his bed and hugged her knees to her chest. *Why were you laughing?*

It's hilarious. How pointless everything is.

Everything isn't pointless.

How could you possibly know that? First there, then the university. Jamie worked as a "knowledge translation specialist" at one of the big universities in the city, which was a fancy way of saying he did graphic and web design for a handful of psychology and sociology professors and edited their write-ups so they were readable. *These people, all these people, they pretend they want to make the world better but all they really care about is their own careers. We get hundreds of thousands of dollars in research funding, supposedly to help the mental health and addiction crisis, just to make shelf art that no one reads, and no one gets helped. It's not even deliberately bullshit; it's just that we don't know any other way to be.*

Forget about work. There are other things that aren't pointless.

Like what?

Friends, family.

You don't even like your family.

Love, she added.

That's all?

That's a lot.

I want to do something meaningful, he said.

Meaning. I can't imagine how philosophers could waste their lives trying to figure out the "meaning" of life—

Pretty self-indulgent.

It's so obvious. The meaning of life is to live it.

He shook his head. *Living isn't meaningful.*

Then let's do something together. We can volunteer with the Suzuki Foundation, we can pick up trash whenever we see it on the ground. We can always smile at people on the street. She was rambling. *We can give money to grassroots charities and homeless people. I think as long as your impact on the world is a positive one, the degree of that impact doesn't matter.*

Jamie was quiet.

How long did you laugh for? Lisa asked. *On the bus.*

I don't know, maybe fifteen minutes. Then after that I didn't feel anything for two years. I thought about killing myself, but I couldn't do that to my mom.

Lisa took his hand. *I think I might love you,* she said. It was the first time she'd said it.

Why? he asked.

I don't know, I just do.

Jamie gave her hand a squeeze. *I think I love you too.*

Years after this conversation, Lisa stumbled across the term "manic pixie dream girl" in a film review. The review argued that manic pixie dream girls—the quirky, unabashedly girlish love interests often seen in movies featuring sulky white male protagonists—were solely a product of the male imagination, but Lisa didn't agree with this. Her theory was that male screenwriters didn't invent the manic pixie dream girl, that's how some women in their lives actually interacted with them. Being around someone who is always sad could put a person in an artificially cheerful state, Lisa thought. You try so hard to be kind, compassionate, patient, and understanding, you tell yourself that they are ill and you tell yourself that you can help and that underneath their coldness and behind every attempt to push you away, they still want you there, you just need to understand them. The problem with these men was that they were so worried about whether the manic pixie dream girl understood them that they never worried enough about whether they understood her.

Lisa realized she had been folding all her hurt and anger and selfishness into a dense knot in her throat. She'd manic-pixie-dream-girled herself.

But the truth was she liked the kindness that was drawn out of her by someone who needed so much of it.

Lisa let her hand fall over her stomach. If she decided to keep the baby, it was her responsibility to let go of her negativity so she wouldn't poison the fetus with all the broken-heart sand. *I'll do anything to make you happy,* she told her daughter silently.

But what if that was impossible? What if she was bringing a child into this world who, like her father, didn't want to live in it? If Lisa had this child, if she stayed with Jamie, was she condemning herself to a life without affection? One where she and her partner rarely left their apartment, had no mutual friends? But one with a partner who was financially stable and kind most of the time and loved her, even though he almost never touched her. It wasn't that bad, she thought, as far as lives went.

Be stronger.

Lower your expectations.

Her throat tightened. She heard the ding of the door to the gallery office, and rose quietly, slipping out the swinging doors to the theatre lobby before Greg could spot her and ask why she wasn't in administration where she belonged. It didn't matter anyway. The gallery had lost its power to calm her.

Look, there's something you must understand. Lisa stood in front of the mirror in the women's washroom, her lips moving soundlessly.

Things are always more complicated than they seem. Take the conflict with Greg. Was this the story of a forty-five-year-old man who had just gotten his first break as a curator at a small-time community art gallery only to discover that in order to fill his predecessor's shoes he'd have to work sixty hours per week instead of the forty he signed up for, or is it the story of a twenty-five-year-old woman in her first arts job after graduation who wanted so badly to believe that the work she was doing writing marketing copy and creating promotional materials was important, was necessary, was worthwhile, that she clung to her love for the job even when it felt like it might destroy her? Who was the protagonist of this conflict? Who was the antagonist? Greg, a man with a chip on his shoulder because he never became an artist, who has a wife and two children under the age of ten, or Lisa, a young woman still discovering her own voice, who was capable of working long hours into the night because part of her never wanted to go home.

The curator before Greg, Ainsley, had been thirty-one and ambitious. She'd created dozens of new programs that kept her at work twelve or thirteen hours per day, which is why she was eventually headhunted for one of the big galleries downtown. Lisa had admired her passion and tried to keep up with it. She'd made herself flexible to missed deadlines and quick turnarounds. She adopted Ainsley's projects as her own. She believed they were doing good, they were bringing art to their community, they were creating opportunities for artists and students.

Greg usually arrived late, took long lunches, and left at 5:00 p.m. on the dot, so he was cutting Ainsley's programs: the after-school workshops, the student film festival, all the gallery publications that used to accompany exhibitions. As far as Greg was concerned, his job was done as long as there was art hanging on the walls. He had twenty years of experience. How dare she tell him how to do his job?

At least that's how Lisa imagined Greg must think, what the story of their conflict must look like from his point of view. She was trying to be more empathetic so she didn't punch him in his lazy face.

The night after Greg announced in a staff meeting that he was cutting the student film festival, Lisa and several of her co-workers went out for Claire's birthday and had too much to drink. (Another reason she drank so much: she'd asked Jamie to come with her and he'd refused because bars stressed him out, and he didn't know these friends anyway. *How are you supposed to get to know my friends if you won't come meet them?* she'd asked.) She'd started crying on her walk home and hadn't been able to stop. She asked herself why she cared so much. It was just a stupid job.

She might have been crying because she was lonely. She had a lot of reasons to cry, she thought, it seemed silly to try to pick one. But when she walked through their door and Jamie asked her what was wrong, she told him all about what had happened at work and that became the truth.

As she fell onto their bed in tears, she said she was depressed.

You're not depressed, moo, he said, running his fingers through her hair. *Shitty things are just happening to you.* Lisa supposed this was true.

The next time Lisa had one of her crying fits around Jamie, she blamed it on work again. Then he caught her again and she did it again, and again. They began bonding over their newly shared hatred for their jobs, the meaninglessness of work, the superficiality and selfishness of their colleagues and of the majority of the population. (She still tried to rally him to go *do something* about it with her. They formed plans to start a magazine, to start a charity-watch website, to start a political comic strip, written by Jamie and illustrated by Lisa. But none of these plans ever became more than conversations. She wondered sometimes if this was her fault, maybe she wasn't pushing him hard enough. Maybe she was an enabler.) She couldn't tell whether or not he believed the things he said. She couldn't tell whether or not she believed the things she said, but the more she said them, the more she needed to say them and the more she hated going to the job she had previously loved. She had decided on her truth: whatever was wrong with her had nothing to do with Jamie.

To tell Jamie about the baby or not?

To keep the baby or not?

To break up or not?

A complication. For the four years of their relationship, Lisa had blamed all of Jamie's difficult traits on his depression: his reluctance to leave the apartment, his unwillingness to spend time with her friends and family, all the hours he spent watching television or playing video games, his low sex drive, the way he sometimes slept twelve or thirteen hours per day. Lisa had always believed that if she could just help Jamie get better, he'd leave the house and spend time with other people—she knew that if he just let people get to know him, they would like him as much as she did. But lately Lisa had realized that she didn't know which traits were Jamie's depression and which traits were just Jamie. Maybe one day he'd be happy, but he'd still be the same.

Another complication—what if she was the problem? Maybe if she got better, Jamie would too.

A third complication—Lisa frequently fantasized about what her and Jamie's children would look like. Would they get his black hair but her blue eyes? Would they be tall and thin like him, or shorter and curvier like her? Their children would be beautiful, she knew that. They would be smart. They would be compassionate. She could love them. That was what she'd always wanted most, after all—someone to love. Someone safe to love. And, she thought, running her hand over her slight belly, she would do everything to make them happy.

She began to cramp and then felt a damp warmness between her legs as she slowly inched her old Honda Civic homeward through the dense rush-hour traffic. Lisa dug her fingertips into the steering wheel. She didn't know how to feel, or what to wish for. She didn't know that it meant anything.

The apartment was empty when she finally got home. Her lower abdomen ached, far worse than her usual period cramps. She rushed through their bedroom and into the bathroom, and pulled down her skirt and underwear. She wasn't surprised to see the blood.

Of course, she thought. She had decided she loved the child. Of course it would leave her.

Without sitting up from the toilet, she leaned over to the bathtub and turned on the hot-water tap.

After her shower, Lisa inserted a pad into a fresh pair of underwear and changed into her pyjamas. She wrapped the clothes she had been wearing into a towel and dropped them in the laundry hamper. She quickly checked the carpet in the bedroom for signs of blood and found none—not a drop of evidence. Lisa swallowed hard and waited, but the tears didn't come. She was fine. She hated herself for that. She had always been such a crybaby and now that something had happened to her that was really worth crying about, she didn't care. Why didn't her body care? Once the thought took root, she realized she could never cry about the miscarriage in front of anyone without it seeming like—and therefore becoming—another performance. Maybe that was unfair. *Maybe everything's performance,* she thought dully. She couldn't let her mouth fill with the words. *Miscarriage. Pregnant. Baby.* It happened and then it unhappened.

When she came out of the bedroom, Jamie was slumped on the couch watching some real-crime-murder-mystery on Netflix she didn't recognize, his skinny bar legs stretched out onto Lisa's yoga ball. He looked up as she closed the door: "Moo?" Over on the shelf near the kitchen sink, the bottles of supplements were lined up in the exact same spots she'd left them days earlier.

The problem was, she loved him, and love wasn't like mould you could cut off a block of cheese to make it good as new, it wasn't a tumour, it wasn't *growth*, it couldn't be removed. Love was an absence; love was rot wearing holes in your heart. Something that had occurred to Lisa in the shower: if the hole created by loving someone isn't filled with their love for you, it can lead to more decay, in the same way a dentist has to fill cavities or they will keep on expanding until the tooth dies. That cavity, that *nothingness* that physically hurt and might even kill you unless it's filled, she thought, that's love.

Lisa knew she was contradicting herself, she was always contradicting herself, but just because some ideas and feelings were incongruous didn't mean they weren't all a little bit true.

Does that make sense? Do you understand?

No, I don't, she answered herself. *Maybe understanding isn't the point.*

"Hey, moo," she said to Jamie.

"You took a shower, moo?"

"Yeah. I was stressed from work."

"Did it help?"

"Yeah," she said. "I think so."

She sat next to him on the couch and leaned in to kiss him on the cheek. "I love you," she said.

Jamie didn't say anything. When she pulled back, she noticed his eyes were red. Her body stiffened in panic, but he kept his eyes on the TV.

"Why?" he asked, after a minute.

Lisa relaxed, a little. He didn't know.

She made herself as small as possible, then pushed her curled body into the cavity formed by his slumped torso until one arm fell slack over her. She started to tell him why she loved him, taking long pauses between each reason to search her brain for an answer he hadn't heard before—one so perfect he might actually start to believe it and be happy.

CAPTAIN
CANADA

Seven years after the divorce, Captain Canada completed construction on the new lake house and invited his family up over the long weekend to celebrate. The cabin—or, as his sister's hand-carved sign dubbed it, *The Fortress of Relaxitude*—was three thousand square feet of house and six thousand square feet of deck hugged by the old-growth rainforest that blanketed the surrounding hills. Down a small flight of wooden stairs, Chloe Canada and her brother Kyle stood at the end of the dock and stared down at the lake, which was as smooth and undisturbed as maple syrup in the dead summer heat.

Captain Canada had bought the lot with his wife, Evelyn, when the twins were toddlers. Five years after they'd separated, she'd sold her half back to him—*I thought if I waited long enough, I could go without becoming sad,* she said to her daughter. *But the smell of the lake reminds me of him. I stare at the walls where we took family photos down.* The sun had bleached the wood around the frames a slightly lighter shade of gold.

Evelyn sold the family house in West Vancouver and used the money to buy a sprawling penthouse overlooking English Bay. *It's like living in a vacation home,* she said. She transferred

Chloe's and Kyle's childhood bedrooms to the new residence without forgetting a single thumbtack. They both thanked their mother for being so considerate, but secretly Chloe had trouble sleeping in her new room. Light came through her old curtains differently, reflected off the walls differently, created new ghosts. When she opened her eyes, everything looked as it should and then it didn't, like she was still trapped within a dream.

Their father had shown no such consideration when it came to the lake—Captain Canada had demolished the old cabin with a single punch, leaving most of the old furniture and artwork inside. It took nearly two years for contractors to remove the rubbish and rebuild.

Kyle pulled the last of the bags from the boat and it bobbed up in gratitude. They had ridden low across the lake, not daring to break five knots in case they hit a wave and went under. Their father refused to take ferries or drive long distances, and had flown, leaving the twins to pack all his clothing and supplies into Kyle's tiny Civic, and then, when he didn't meet them at the public dock or answer his cellphone, into the rusted skiff they'd borrowed from a neighbour.

"Do you think he hit a plane?" Chloe asked. "Or one of the mountains. Or a flock of birds." Captain Canada wore thick goggles when he flew, but if he smoked a 747, there would be no survivors. He was strong, sure, but lots of things were strong. An ant could balance forty-nine other ants on its back, but it would still die if you crushed it with a rock.

She knelt to pick up a flat of beer, but struggled under the weight. Neither Kyle nor Chloe had any sort of powers; the radiation poisoning that had given Captain Canada his Herculean abilities had failed to super-heroize his sperm.

Kyle shook his head. "He's probably just busy."

Chloe's left hand slipped and, before she could catch it, a bottle tipped off the flat and rolled onto the dock and into the water. She steadied herself and watched the bottle sink until it blinked out like a twinkle in an eye. "Shit," she said.

"Don't worry about it, Dad can fish it out later," Kyle said. "Christ, put that down before you hurt yourself. Leave the heavy stuff for Dad."

"I'm fine." She teetered along the dock and started up the stairs. "Who knows how long he'll be?"

Eight years ago, her mother had come home at midnight with salt stains on her favourite red dress and a strand of seaweed tangled in her long black hair. She'd thrown open the door to Chloe's bedroom and plucked the novel she was reading from her hands. *You are beautiful, strong, and intelligent,* Evelyn had said, cupping Chloe's face in her thin hands, *you can save yourself.* Evelyn meant it as an affirmation, but as she slipped into sleep, Chloe curled up around her—at twelve, she was already taller and heavier, and this was the first time it occurred to her she could be the armour that protected her mother instead of the other way around—and whispered back, *I promise.*

Chloe heard the roar of the engine long before she saw the speedboat dart across the lake toward them.

They walked down to meet the boat as it rounded an inflatable party island and three-pointed in to the dock. Their aunt Noemi waved from the bow. Captain Canada lounged behind the wheel, naked except for his maple-leaf swim trunks and a pair of mirrored sunglasses. Noemi's husband and children, Tony and Ally, sprawled out on the seats behind him. In the passenger's seat, Captain Canada's manager sat cross-legged in professional white shorts and a loose red tank top, rapidly typing something onto her phone. Christina was in her late thirties but looked much younger. She had protected herself with a wide-brimmed hat and a thick layer of sunscreen that made her pale olive skin glow. Chloe could barely see Christina beneath the hat, only her skinny elbows jutting out on either side like the leaves of a flower.

Captain Canada sprung out of the boat and almost flipped the dock when he landed on it. Chloe grabbed Kyle's forearm for balance. "We called you," she said. "We were calling you."

"Sorry about that, honey." He tousled her hair and laughed.

She batted him away. "Are you drunk?"

Christina stood and turned her phone toward the twins. "Check it out, we ran into a group whose boat broke down. We already have two hundred retweets."

On the screen, Captain Canada caught a rainbow ski rope and hooked the triangular handle around his shoulder. He started to run across the water, towing a small party boat with a dozen twentysomethings behind him. They had their hands in the air to toast him with beer cans and cellphones. One girl—a bottle blond in an orange bikini—tossed him a can of Canadian, which he caught, drank, and tossed back in a single motion. After five or six seconds, the video looped and Captain Canada caught the rope again, hooked the handle again, caught the beer again, saved the day again.

"Oh man," Kyle said. "They should offer you an endorsement."

"Pretty sick, right?" Tony clambered out of the boat. "Folks were super-chill. Al, throw the rope." He secured the boat as his family spilled out onto the dock.

"We lost track of time! Were you waiting long? How'd you get over?" Noemi swept Chloe up in an enormous hug. Like her younger brother, Noemi was tall, strong, dark-haired, and tan. Chloe always felt very small with her father's family. She was a half-foot shorter than her aunt and brother and Ally, and nearly a foot shorter than Tony and her father. Her father's arms were thicker than her legs.

Captain Canada lifted the skiff over his head and took off across the lake to return it to its owner. Chloe lifted a hand to shield her eyes from the orange glow of the late afternoon sun, watching the ripples spread where her father's feet had glanced off the water. Next to her, Tony cracked open another beer, and one-handed Kyle toward the edge of the dock. Kyle staggered forward but caught himself before he went over.

"The hell, man? My phone's in my pocket."

Tony laughed and jumped into the lake feet-first, submerging and emerging with his beer held proudly above the water like an Olympic torch.

Chloe felt like her family was dancing to a beat she couldn't quite catch. The lonely feeling she'd had in the forty-five minutes they'd been missing hadn't gone away the way she'd expected it to when the boat brought them back.

"Why the long face?" her father asked as he landed on the deck.

"You shouldn't drive the boat when you've been drinking," she said.

He laughed and disappeared inside the cabin. He returned with a large knife and handed it to Chloe handle-first. "Here." He leapt backward. "Throw it at me."

"What?"

"Throw it at me."

"Are you kidding? No."

"I'm serious, honey, just throw it at me."

"Dad, I'm not going to throw a knife at you!"

"Son! What about you?"

Kyle glanced up from the game of cribbage he was playing with Ally. He laid his cards face-down on the table and put his beer on top of them. "What's up?"

"Take the knife from your sister and throw it at me."

Kyle shrugged and stood. Chloe narrowed her eyes at her brother and tightened her grip. They'd spent every second together in the womb and had grown more and more apart every year since they'd slipped out of it. He took the knife from her and flung it as hard as he could. A year ago, Chloe thought, he would have been on her side. Then she realized: a year ago, she probably would have thrown the knife.

Captain Canada caught it by the handle when the blade was less than an inch from his nose. "Even drunk," he said, juggling the knife in one hand carelessly, "my reflexes are a thousand times faster than a normal man's."

"It's not your reflexes, it's your judgment," Chloe said, but no one seemed to hear her.

He pointed to one of the taller, thicker trees past the far side of the deck. "Wanna bet I can hit that tree? Kyle? Ally?"

"No one's going to bet you, Uncle C. We all know you can do it."

"Five bucks says you can't stick the blade," said Kyle.

He did it on the second try.

Over on the table, Chloe's cellphone buzzed. She picked it up and saw a text message from Evelyn: *How is it?*

It was a trap. Positive or negative, there was absolutely nothing Chloe could say that would not upset her mother. She pondered over her answer, then showed her phone to Kyle. After a moment, he typed *it's okay* and hit send, then went back to his game.

Tony disappeared and reappeared about half an hour later with three girls who looked around nineteen or twenty. Chloe recognized the girl in the orange bikini from the video—she had thrown Captain Canada the beer as he towed their party boat to shore.

Tony bounced across the deck with a huge grin and disappeared inside the cabin. Chloe lowered her book when she heard her father's voice bellow out the door—"Of course! The more the merrier!"

Tony emerged with Kyle and four fistfuls of beer bottles. "Ladies! To the floaty!" The Party Boat Girls cheered and all five of them padded back down to the dock. Chloe watched as

Tony and Kyle distributed the beers, and they jumped in the water and swam over to the island float.

She dropped her book on the lounge, stood, and walked into the cabin. Inside, Aunt Noemi aggressively chopped vegetables. Christina was at the kitchen table, hunched over a stack of papers with a pen jutting out of the side of her mouth.

"Where'd Dad go?"

"He went to the store to pick up a few more steaks," Noemi said.

Chloe sidled up to her. "Does that mean they're staying for dinner, then?"

"I imagine so."

She peered up at Noemi and noted with relief that her aunt appeared irritated about her son's guests.

"Do you need help?" Chloe asked.

"No, thank you," Christina answered. Her pen tumbled from her lips and clicked down on the table. Then she sat straight up. "Oh! I'm sorry. Not me. Sorry. It's hard, finding time to go through this with Danny."

Danny. Chloe had thought the only people who called him that anymore were Noemi and his mother. Even Evelyn referred to him as *Captain Canada* or *your father*. "No worries," Chloe said, her throat tight.

Noemi handed her the knife. "Chop large. We're roasting them on the barbecue." She went over to the stove to attend to the croutons.

"What are you working on?" Chloe asked.

Christina flitted through the papers. "Licensing agreements. We're meeting with the lawyer next week. Twenty-five years and no action figures, no movies? He's getting older.

What does super-speed do with cancer? What does super-strength do with arthritis?"

"Or Alzheimer's," Noemi interjected.

"That's a long way off," Chloe said.

"I know," Christina said. "But there's something to be said about an early retirement."

"For sure." Chloe slid the knife through a zucchini, again, and again. She paused. "Kyle could write a movie."

"Hmm?"

"That's what he's studying at UBC—writing and journalism. He's really good. He's had a few stories published."

"Hmm." Christina said again. "That's interesting." She popped her pen back in her mouth.

Chloe felt a fresh wave of rage wash over her and stick to her skin like salt. "So what do you guys think of the new cabin?" she baited them both.

"I love it," Christina said at the same time Noemi said, "It's nice."

"It's very elegant, classy," Christina continued.

"Yes, it is," Noemi agreed. "But I liked the old cabin too. It was homey, it had character."

"I miss it," Chloe said, her voice an octave higher than normal. She watched the back of her aunt's head as she walked over to the fridge and pulled out a head of lettuce and took it to the sink. She looked for signs that Noemi understood that in the eight years since he had moved out of their house, barely a conversation passed where Evelyn did not mention Captain Canada. That when her mother asked *how is it?* she meant *has anyone mentioned me?*

Her mother and her aunt had been close once, but after the divorce Captain Canada filled the space between them and expanded. At first, they met weekly. Then monthly. And then only at events hosted by mutual friends, where they stood close together, clinked their wineglasses, and promised to meet up again soon. Once, Chloe's mother had a glass too many and said *I miss you.* Chloe had been seventeen or eighteen, and when she overheard she couldn't tell whether Evelyn was speaking to her former sister-in-law or her former husband, who was off saving lives after some natural disaster, and also, as always, standing between them.

There was a light thud as Captain Canada landed on the deck.

"Me too," Noemi said placidly.

A year earlier, as Evelyn drove Chloe across the country to McGill, she'd brought up the night before the separation—the night she'd crawled into bed with her daughter with seaweed in her hair.

You know, she said, *your father used to rescue me a lot.*

It was true. Evelyn had been a regular Mary Jane/Lois Lane/five-foot-two-ninety-pound-damsel-in-distress. She'd been in and out of hostage situations and in and out of hospitals all throughout Chloe's childhood.

They were at a restaurant a few blocks from their hotel. *He was only ever there for me when I needed help,* she said. *He wouldn't be there for coffee or for dinner or for watching TV. He was the sun and I was the moon, and it was like I disappeared from the sky when he wasn't looking,* she said. *When he went away, he didn't even miss me.*

She bent forward and stared at her daughter through her wineglass. *Do you understand?*

Chloe was old enough and well-read enough to recognize the metaphor, and was vaguely disappointed in her mother for using it. *I think so,* she said. She wondered why, in every story, in every song, the sun was male and the moon was female. People were greater than that, she thought, people were suns and moons and black holes all at once, emitting their own light while reflecting and absorbing the light of others. The whole world pulsed with their energies.

Evelyn's words echoed through Chloe's head as she took her plate and wineglass and squeezed her chair up to join her family and Tony's Party Boat Girls at the table on the deck. She let her sunglasses fall from her forehead over her eyes. Noemi stood as Chloe sat. "I'd like to thank my brother. For generously hosting us here this weekend."

Everyone raised their glass. Chloe hesitated and glanced across the table at her brother. Kyle had his wineglass in the air. She quickly lifted hers.

"To Captain Canada!"

"To Dad!" Chloe and Kyle said in unison. Kyle met her eyes and smiled.

The night before he left, I'd had enough. We were on a gala cruise, with local politicians and celebrities. It was my idea. I didn't want to go, but I thought I could get him *to go, do you understand? But he ignored me the whole night. It was windy, and English Bay was rough. I was standing next to a railing and I lost my balance.* At this, Evelyn had paused. *I could have caught myself, but I didn't. I let the wind carry me over.*

Mom?

No. I jumped.

Mom.

I fell. And then I was in the ocean. I thrashed about and waited for him to come save me. But he never did. He didn't even notice I was gone. So I swam to shore. I never needed him to save me.

No, Chloe said, but she wasn't sure she believed it.

You're going to be alone for the first time in your life, Evelyn said. *I want you to remember this: you'll be fine.*

She had reached across the table and hugged her daughter. *You'll be great.*

Chloe realized she was muttering her mother's words—*I never needed him to save me, you're going to be alone*—and sucked her lips to her teeth to stop them from tumbling out. Kyle's eyes were still locked on her. He wrinkled his brow and shook his head slightly.

Chloe paused for a moment, then mouthed the words *it's nothing* and dropped her wine to her lips.

As Noemi settled into her seat, Ally stood and raised her glass again. "And to Mom! For preparing this wonderful meal!"

"To Noemi!"

They began to dig in.

After a few bites, the Party Boat Girl in the orange bikini stood. "To Captain Canada!" she shouted.

Everyone raised their glasses again. "To Captain Canada!"

Chloe could barely take her eyes off her plate.

At the end of the meal, as Chloe pushed her chair out to help clear the plates, she noticed that underneath the table, Christina's knee rested against her father's.

She barrelled into the kitchen and dumped her dishes in the sink. She was in the middle of yanking open the dishwasher when Tony popped his head in. "We're going out in the boat!" he shouted.

Chloe kicked the dishwasher door back into place and followed him outside. The Party Boat Girls had shed their sundresses on the deck and were plucking beach towels from the clothesline. Ally pulled a wetsuit over her bikini. Captain Canada had his foot to an air pump quick as a hummingbird, blowing up one towable tube and then two more in under a minute. The nylon covers were bright red with twin lightning bolts wrapped around each side and a deranged-looking smiley face scrawled across the top.

Christina appeared beside her. "You like them? The clerk said they were the best for speed and getting air." She said the last two words as though they were in a foreign language.

"Who's driving?" Chloe said.

Kyle rounded the cabin with a small beer cooler. Captain Canada stacked the three tubes on top of each other and lifted them with one hand. The Party Boat Girl in the orange bikini bounded up to him. "Can you carry me too?" she trilled.

Chloe watched Christina's face, but her gaze had dropped back down to her phone and she betrayed no emotion.

Captain Canada nodded and crouched with his free hand palm-up at her knees. She gingerly stepped onto his hand one foot at a time, clutching a fistful of his hair for support.

"Careful!" Chloe called out. "His hair's not nearly as sturdy as it once was."

They both turned toward her. "You brat," he said with a half-grin. "You coming?"

"You sure it's a good idea to take the boat out now?"

"For sure," Tony said. "We only got like ninety minutes of light left."

"That's not what I meant."

"Watch your balance." Captain Canada hoisted Orange Bikini into the air. "Come on now, Miss Sober," he said to Chloe. "I'll need a good spotter."

Tony, Kyle, Ally, and the other two Party Boat Girls were already staggered along the stairs. Through the trees, Chloe could see her aunt and uncle waiting on the dock below. All at once, the whole lot looked back up at the cabin, and even though Chloe knew it was ridiculous, she could swear they were all looking straight at her. The evening sun beat down and cast a golden glow on them. A teardrop of sweat shivered down her spine.

"Uncle C!" Tony shouted. "Hurry it up!"

"Coming?" he asked her.

"Yeah." She started toward the stairs. Her father stepped behind her with unusual care, his arms extended with their loads like a human scale. It reminded Chloe of a picture of her parents that had hung in the old cabin: they were both in their early twenties, and she sat on his shoulder with his arm fastened firmly around her calves. Her arms and fingers were extended, jazz-handed, while his other arm was bent, his palm spread like a falling star. His face was turned up to hers and hers down to his. He smiled while she laughed. It had been taken the summer after they'd both graduated from the University of British Columbia—him in engineering, and her in political science—and one year before the accident turned Danny Cordano into the country's most-beloved superhero. Chloe realized with a jolt that the photo had probably been carted away with the wreckage.

Down at the dock, Kyle, Tony, and Ally jumped aboard the tubes. Tony grinned up at the Party Boat Girls as they piled into the back of the boat. "We'll show you how it's done."

Chloe took the seat behind her father, facing the stern. She nudged the beer cooler open with her bare foot and bent down to grab an apple cider. On the dock, Aunt Noemi untied the last rope and jumped into the hull next to her husband. Captain Canada started the engine and inched the boat out into the open water. Once the tubes were clear, he turned the boat sharp left, straightened out, and gunned it, yanking the tubers up over the wake and into the air.

He jerked the wheel right as they landed, skipping the three tubes out of the wake until they were almost perpendicular to the boat. As they flung back to the wake, Kyle grabbed the side handle of Tony's tube and held on until the last second, sending him flying over the wave and skyward. The tube tilted, and Tony's legs and torso hinged up away from it, but he kept his death grip on the front handles and shifted his weight mid-air to land with only a slight bounce. The Party Boat Girls gasped, and Orange Bikini snapped a series of pictures and eagerly showed her phone to the others. Chloe took another drink and let her gaze drift down to the screen. Orange Bikini had impeccable timing—she'd caught all three in the air, their faces frozen, mouths open between fear and joy.

Orange Bikini leaned across the boat and put a hand on Captain Canada's arm. She said something Chloe couldn't hear over the sound of wind and waves and the Blue Rodeo song Noemi blasted through the boat's speakers from her iPod. He looked at the photo and laughed. Chloe wanted to rip the other girl's hand away from her father. He was more than twice her fucking age. Chloe would not have been surprised to learn this girl was on the wrong side of a high school diploma. She wanted to tell her that Captain-fucking-Canada hadn't taken three whole days off to entertain an insipid celebrity-worshipper with greasy roots. That in all likelihood, somewhere someone had died because Captain Canada wasn't there to save them.

After all, wasn't that the whole point? Every birthday, every hockey game, every anniversary, their high school graduation, Kyle's reading at the university, every dinner, every breakfast, every weekend morning—how many lives were they willing to sacrifice so he could be there for them?

Shortly before the divorce, she and Kyle and their mother had watched an interview with Captain Canada on *The Hour*.

I love it, he said. *I'm anxious when I'm not working. I worry. I love my country, I love my world. I love everyone in it. I know I can't save everyone.* George Stroumboulopoulos nodded sympathetically. *But I can do my best.* Applause. Canada's hero smiled graciously at the camera.

Chloe had wondered whether there was someone out there who wouldn't get rescued because Captain Canada was at the CBC.

That's bullshit, Evelyn said. *If you love everyone in the world, that's the same as loving no one at all.*

How selfish we are, Chloe thought, to want him to love us more.

Captain Canada turned the boat again and sent all three tubes flying across the wake. Tony extended his foot sideways as Kyle zipped toward him, preparing a frog-leg kick.

Chloe swallowed the rest of her cider and bent down to grab another from the cooler.

The Party Boat Girls gasped. Chloe lifted her head. Kyle's tube was bouncing, dragging down at the front where it connected with the rope. Kyle was nowhere to be seen.

"Cut!" she said. "Kyle's off!"

Captain Canada cut the engine and then Chloe saw the blood, saw Kyle's knee and toes jut out from the water in front of the tube.

"*Dad!*" she screamed.

She watched, frozen, as Ally and Tony threw off their life jackets and jumped in the lake. But Captain Canada got there first. He gently pushed the tube off of Kyle, and unlooped the rope from the tube, and then from Kyle's ankle. He cradled his son in his arms and slowly rose into the air.

"Holy shit!"

Kyle's right foot dangled by a bloodied thread. The rope had burnt through to the bone. He wrapped his arms around his father and screamed into his bare shoulder.

Captain Canada glided over to the boat. His face was stone, but his eyes shone—with lake water or tears, Chloe couldn't tell.

"Pass the towel," he said.

One of the Party Boat Girls threw the towel she was sitting on up to Captain Canada. He caught it with one hand and wrapped it around the severed ankle. "Kyle? Son, I need you to hold this." He wrapped his arm back around Kyle, hugging him against his chest.

Chloe stood. "Kyle!" she cried.

"I know it hurts, son. I need you to be brave. I need you to let go of me. I need you to hold the towel."

After a moment, Kyle nodded into his father's shoulder and released his hands. He bent himself toward his foot and firmly clasped his hands on either side of his ankle, around the towel.

"Close your eyes."

And then, like a speeding bullet, Captain Canada and Kyle shot up into the sky and disappeared on the other side of the mountains.

"Kyle!" Chloe angled her way to the hull, elbowing a Party Boat Girl out of her path. She vaulted onto the seat between her aunt and uncle, and then to the tip of the bow and leapt.

For a second, she hovered, like she might be able to follow them, but then she fell straight down into the lake.

As she sunk, she opened her eyes slowly.

Sunbeams and shadows spun around her like the striped top of a carousel. When she looked down, the rays circled into a dark pupil, as if a giant were pinching all the light in the world between his thumb and finger hundreds of kilometres below. She stopped sinking after a couple metres and hovered, held still in the lake's embrace. She'd never felt more loved.

She held her breath for as long as she could, then kicked and clawed her way back to the surface.

LIGHTHOUSE
PARK

When I was eleven and my sister, Courtney, was thirteen, I caught her crying in her bedroom because someone at school called her a wallflower. She didn't know the word, and mistook it for a compliment until she looked it up on our computer. Since then, I've heard a few people at our high school call her that, but even though she was introverted and preferred books to people, I don't think it fit. Courtney was blunt, with a quiet but acerbic wit that was too surprising and too clever to really offend. She spoke quickly and passionately about things she cared about, with an urgency that suggested her world would end if you didn't share her enthusiasm. She was a straight-A student who never hid how smart she knew she was. Four years later, I still honestly don't know what upset her more—that someone had called her a wallflower or that she didn't know what the word meant.

I think the only reason anyone ever mistook Courtney for a wallflower was because she was best friends with Jenny. Jenny was in every school play, while Courtney volunteered to help build and paint the sets. She went on the best adventures, told the best stories, while Courtney laughed in all the right places. She was the star of the girls' rugby team, a fixture at the best parties, loud and vivacious, tall and beautiful, openly queer and confident as hell about it because everyone who knew her was a little bit in love with Jenny, regardless of their sexual orientation. I think the strength of Jenny's light made it easy to mistake Courtney for a moon, instead of a different type of star.

Some people think I should be angry with Jenny—and with Adam, Sophie, Amy, and Ryan…heck, with the whole graduating class of West Vancouver Secondary if I want—because of what happened. They think it's weird we've become such good friends. The thing is, I'm not sure Jenny and I really are friends. We were drawn together by a shared grief and a paralyzing, aimless guilt that erodes us like the ocean. We're more like camp friends than actual friends; we happened to be in the same place at the same time, without many other options. Mostly, we just hang out at Jenny's parents' place and drink.

At school, Jenny and I don't really hang out. Because she's two years older, we don't have any classes together, and at lunch she sits in a stairwell with all of her old friends—Courtney's friends—while I jog down to the beach and back, sometimes twice. I tell anyone who asks that I'm training for Midget AAA tryouts next summer, but the truth is I have no chance at the team. I'm what my coach calls "tenacious," which basically means I'm not big enough to be a goon and not technically skilled enough to be a star. I run because I can't sit still, it's excruciating. I run until my lungs ache, and then I keep going. I run like I'm trying to break free of my body.

The other day, Ryan Mann told me Courtney had a reputation for getting too drunk at parties and making out with random boys.

"It never went further than that," Jenny says when I ask her about it. It's 8:00 p.m. on a Friday night and we're in her bedroom, sharing a bottle of Pinot gris. The walls are papered with posters of Lady Gaga, Tegan and Sara, Janelle Monae, Florence + the Machine, and some older bands like Blondie and Hole. Her clothes and homework and a few empties are in piles on the floor. We sit on the bed and pull straight from the bottle. There's a party down the street that Jenny wants to go to, but I'm not sure.

"They'd call or message her afterwards, you know, and she always turned them down."

The more I think about it, the more this makes sense. Courtney had been best one-on-one. In big groups, she usually found one person willing to have a long conversation with her. It made sense that in a house overflowing with hundreds of drunk teenagers, the person she'd have the easiest time engaging with would be some overly hormonal guy who probably assumed from my sister's intensity that she was also interested, that they were having a moment.

"Pass the bottle if you aren't going to drink." Jenny always outdrinks me three to one. "God, you're such a lightweight."

"I'm sixteen," I say. "I'd be more concerned if I could hold my alcohol, fuck you very much."

"Christine, you aren't even sixteen," she says.

I stick my tongue out at her. I turn sixteen next month, in May. Besides, Jenny has a skewed perception of how often I drink, since I only ever drink when I'm with her. That sounds bad, but it's not a peer-pressure thing (not entirely). I just don't go out all that much. A lot of the things I used to enjoy, such as—in the words of Alison, my grief counsellor—"inter-acting with peers," started to feel exhausting and pointless after Courtney died. I think she's overreacting. I still see people at school, and I started playing hockey again in January. Plus Jenny. There's only so much peer interaction a person can take.

Jenny tilts the bottle back to finish the wine. When she lowers it, her eyes are a little too bright.

"Are you okay?" I ask.

Jenny reaches under the bed for a second bottle and swings it like a mallet into my open hands. "Drink up! Come on, we're going to party tonight!" She leans in, excited. "I hear Hunter got a keg."

I hesitate for a second, then unscrew the cap and drink. I developed from books and movies a romantic notion of drinking as being emblematic of severe emotional problems, like the most hard-core depression and loneliness. I'm not sure whether my desire to get drunk with Jenny all the time is rooted in actual sadness or in my fucked-up need to demonstrate how sad I am by cultivating an aura of fucked-upness. Which is more fucked-up? I wonder.

Jenny completely buys into the "drink to forget" thing. Half the time she's the life of the party, and the other half we wind up going home early because she can't stop crying in the bathroom. She'll probably buy me a dangerous amount of keg beer tonight because she thinks that's helpful. Maybe it is.

"I don't know if I want to go," I say.

"Fuck that. You wouldn't look that cute if you didn't want to go."

Hunter's house is packed by the time we get there. It's two bucks for a Dixie cup of beer; Jenny drags me straight to the line, where a hulking athlete in a pink polo gives us the "rugby" discount of half off. "This doesn't mean I'll chest-bump you, Andy!" Jenny shouts as we walk away. My cup is filled to the brim, and I quickly drink enough to be able to carry it safely, which is almost a third of the cup, because I'm pretty dizzy from all the wine.

Jenny grabs my arm and steers me toward a gangly, emo-core guy with thick-rimmed glasses and stretched ears. "Hunter!" She hugs him. "Great party, thanks for the invite. This is my friend, Christine. Christine, this is Hunter, party host and yearbook photographer, so be nice to him."

"I knew you were using me for my photos."

She grins and sticks a hand on his head to mess up his hair. He ducks and looks annoyed, but in an exaggerated way, for show.

"Nice to meet you," I say, and stick out my hand awkwardly.

I'm relieved when he shakes it. "Likewise."

Jenny disappears and I spin, eventually spotting her hugging and laughing with a group of girls on the other side of the room.

"So how do you know Jenny?"

I turn back to Hunter. "Childhood friends," I say.

"So 'friends' then?"

I realize he's hitting on me, or trying to. "Yeah," I say.

"Do you go to our school? You look familiar."

"I'm in Grade 10."

His eyes widen. "Oh shit, are you—"

"Where's your bathroom?" I cut him off before he can finish.

He points toward the front hall. "There's one next to the laundry room, but if that's busy, go up the stairs, second door on your left."

I head up the stairs and lock myself in the bathroom.

There's a popular myth that you can't fold a piece of paper in half more than seven times. But in theory, if the paper is big enough, you could actually keep folding past seven. If you folded a piece of paper forty-two times, it would reach the moon. One hundred and three times and it could stretch ninety-three billion light years, farther than the universe itself.

I imagine folding into myself again and again until my molecules are stacked single file across the known universe.

After I pee, I sit on the toilet for a long time, waiting to feel like myself again.

Courtney died last August during the biggest party of the year at West Van: the annual Grade 12 camp-out. Courtney's class was one of the few that didn't hike up Cypress Mountain, instead opting to drive to Lighthouse Park and throw the party in a clearing along the main trail, about halfway between the parking lot and the water. I've spent the last eight months trying to piece together the details. (The witnesses were not reliable.) This is what I know: at some point Courtney, Jenny, and four of their friends—Adam Riley, Sophie Wong, Amy Knight, and Ryan Mann—left the party to hike farther down the trail. They smoked a joint on the side of a cliff, overlooking the ocean. In the police report,

Amy described that moment as beautiful. I was also up late that night, at home, reading. My curtains were pulled open and I remember thinking the moon was unusually huge and the stars were unusually bright.

After they ground the remains of the joint into a rock, Adam and Jenny decided to go swimming, and Sophie, who had a crush on Adam, decided to join them. All three stripped down to their underwear and navigated the precarious path down to the water with the help of their cellphones. Up top, Ryan dared Amy and Courtney to shotgun a beer. Then, according to Ryan and Amy, Courtney said she had to go to the bathroom and she slipped off into the woods.

When the cops asked them how much time had passed from the moment Courtney left them until Adam, Jenny, and Sophie came back up the side of the cliff, Ryan answered *a couple of minutes* and Amy said *half an hour*. They'd started making out a few seconds after Courtney left. Neither of them thought to go looking for Courtney, or even missed her, until the others came back up, and Jenny, in the middle of pulling on her jeans, asked where she was.

I hear cheers as I go down the stairs and into the living room, and when I get there, Jenny's doing a keg stand. The girl holding her left leg is Sophie Wong. I wonder if Sophie ever managed to hook up with Adam.

At Courtney's funeral, Sophie had come up and hugged me. *I'm so sorry*, she said.

I told her it wasn't her fault—she'd looked for Courtney, they all had. I said that to a lot of people that night.

I know, I know, she said. *I meant, I'm sorry she's gone.*

She's laughing as she helps Jenny to her feet, in her short skirt and tank top, and at that moment I hate her for being the sort of person who laughs in a tank top.

Jenny has both arms extended like she's directing traffic, accepting high-fives from all sides. The next thing I know, she's at my side, her arms thrown over my shoulders.

"Steen, where have you been?" she slurs. Life of the party, Jenny tonight, apparently.

I push her off. "The fuck did you bring me here for, Jenny? Just to ditch me."

"What? I thought you'd have fun." Her eyes are panicked, unfocused. "Aren't you having fun?"

"Total blast."

Jenny digs a fist into her temple. "Why do you always say that?" she asks. "Why'd you come anyway?"

It's a good question. I can't answer it. "I don't know," I finally say. "I guess I just wanted to hang out with you." I say this as cruelly as possible.

Jenny stares at me like she can see through every last molecule of my bullshit. I'm trying not to cry, struggling to keep my breath even. Then she leans in and locks her lips on mine, pushing me back against the wall.

They found Courtney's shoes on a boulder at the edge of the cliff, her socks balled in the toes, her purse resting against them. Her body, fully clothed, was recovered the next morning from the water below. She had a blood alcohol level of 0.20, otherwise known as "fucking wasted."

There was no note, no obvious warning signs. When the cops came to break the news to us, Dad flat-out denied that Courtney had a history of any mental health problems and I sat on our couch and hugged my knees and didn't say anything. They figured Courtney must have decided to join her friends in the water, that she was drunk and it was too dark for her to see the rocks below. Lighthouse Park is famous for cliff jumping, after all.

The *North Shore News* described it as a tragic accident.

I'm too surprised to push Jenny away. My hand has found its way to her shoulder, as if by instinct. I hear boys holler in the background, shouting words of encouragement.

Jenny jerks her head back. "Christine, I—"

But then she's cut off by Phil Rogers, who stumbles past us, double-fisting two Dixie cups. "Next best thing, eh?" he says to Jenny.

Before she can say anything, I launch myself at him, slamming my shoulder into his torso so he hits the wall, spilling beer everywhere. It hurts. A lot. More than I expect; I have never bodychecked anyone without shoulder pads before, let alone a guy who easily has fifty pounds on me. But he's so drunk and so surprised he loses his balance and crumples to the ground. I feel rage surge through me, like lava poured into my veins. I'd learned in first-aid courses that it was dangerous to drink in a hot tub or sauna because heat quickens the effects of alcohol. Maybe rage did the same. Maybe that's where the expression *makes your blood boil* comes from.

The world pinches in, and I start kicking and kicking, until someone—I don't see who—grabs me and pulls me back. I flail. Once I start crying I won't be able to stop. I break out of their arms and tear through the party, out to the street, and I run. I run like I'm trying to leave my body behind me.

I don't get far. I start crying after a few blocks and my lungs cannot bear both burdens, so I slow to a jog, then a walk. I realize I'm lost, and how ridiculous it is to be lost when you have a mountain as a landmark, and then I realize I left my purse at the party and I decide I don't care.

I hear someone shout my name. When I turn around, Jenny's jogging to catch up to me.

"Hey," she says.

"Hey."

"Are you okay?"

I shake my head. "That's such a stupid fucking question."

"I'm sorry—I, uh," she laughs a little. "Yeah, it's a pretty stupid fucking question."

She hands me my purse and we start walking.

"Thanks."

"This way," she says, steering us back to her house. Within a block we're back in an area I recognize, and I'm a little disappointed.

"Is Phil okay?"

"Oh god, yeah, he's fine. Just bruised and pissed off. Hey, look," she says, looking at her feet instead of me. "He was sort of right, you know? Not that you're the next best thing—he's an asshole—I mean, the kiss wasn't about you."

"Yeah," I say.

"I'm really sorry, that was—I shouldn't have."

"It's okay," I say.

Jenny's family lives in an aging house in Ambleside, about a twenty-minute walk from the condo I share with my dad. We go around the back to Jenny's bedroom door and let ourselves in, as quietly as possible. The walls and floors in Jenny's house are paper-thin. You can hear a mouse dart across the top floor from the basement, and the whole house shudders whenever someone uses the stairs or flushes a toilet. Her great-grandfather built the place shortly after the Lions Gate Bridge opened. He died a couple of months after his wife, the same year Jenny was born—of a broken heart, according to Jenny, and when she told me that I had gone home and pressed my ear against my dad's chest, only to realize I didn't know the difference between the sound of a healthy heart and a broken one.

She rolls a joint and smokes it out the window. "It helps me sleep," she says. She's told me this a million times, with an edge to her voice like she's waiting for me to agree with her. I want to ask if she thinks the self-destructive shit she started doing a little too much since Courtney's death is performative at all, but decide against it. If Jenny's overthinking every little thing the same way I am, she isn't letting on, and I've heard weed makes some people paranoid and I don't want to wreck the mood.

We order the vegetarian special from Hot Slice, pay the delivery guy in loonies and fives, and sit on Jenny's bed and watch an old comedy on Netflix. We know every line and we laugh seconds before each joke. It's my favourite part of these nights—curling up in Jenny's bed with her laptop, watching half of a movie we've both seen too many times, falling asleep with a pizza box at our feet. It's something Courtney and I used to do, and even though Jenny—who is big-boned, blond, and beautiful—bears little physical resemblance to my tiny, dark-haired sister, there's a blurry point just before I pass out from alcohol and exhaustion where I can almost believe it's Courtney I'm curled up next to, not Jenny.

I wonder if Jenny imagines the same thing. I think she must, but I know we'll never talk about it.

As the credits roll, I flip the laptop shut and put it on the floor. Jenny grunts as I settle in on my side of the bed. I stare at a framed photo on Jenny's desk—it's too dark to make out more than shadows, but I've memorized my sister's tight-lipped smile. She and Jenny are eight or nine in the photo, dressed for Halloween. Jenny is Wonder Woman, punching the camera. Courtney is Katniss Everdeen, her bow dangling at her hip. I can hear her laughing, cautious and tense, her joy butting up against her sealed lips and failing to fully escape.

"Jenny," I whisper. "Do you think she was happy?"

She takes so long to answer I'm sure she's asleep. Then: "I don't know."

I picture her shoes, her socks, her purse. Stacked so neatly, waiting for her.

Jenny's breaths get slow and heavy with sleep. I close my eyes, and follow.

ANHEDONIA

Patient Zero had always been an unhappy man, and because of this, no one would ever be exactly sure when and how the virus began.

His wife drove him to the emergency room when the whites of his eyes turned a deep, uniform red. When his fever rose above 104 degrees and he began to vomit blood, he was transferred to infectious diseases and placed under quarantine. When the doctor told his wife they didn't think he would make it—the dehydration was too severe, the weight and blood loss too great—she didn't react. She said she didn't feel anything, other than a headache.

Rattled, the doctor went to lie down for a few minutes in the on-call room and didn't get up for an hour. That evening, she told her husband of three months that she felt "blue," and declined to have sex.

Soon her eyes turned red.

Two days later, Patient Zero died, and dozens more presenting with the same symptoms were admitted to hospitals across Greater Vancouver. A phone call came in about a similar case in Toronto, and another in Beijing. In LA, a young actor was hospitalized after walking off the edge of a bridge, and when asked about his medical history, he swore up and down that no, he had never been depressed before, but he had just returned from Vancouver. His eyes turned red the next day, and newspapers across the globe broke the story: there was a new pandemic, and the first symptom was debilitating anhedonia.

*

Maureen De Luca @maureendelooka
Hey, so I've been AWOL and caught up on news after four days. Can anyone on here update/clarify? I'm in #YVR, is it safe to leave my apartment?

Dave Jamieson @davejj1985
@maureendelooka If you're healthy & safe, stay put. Shove towels under your door. Block your vents. Especially in YVR. Think this is the end

Emily D @emdearly
@davejj1985 @maureendelooka This is fear-mongering.

Dave Jamieson @davejj1985
@emdearly @maureendelooka Businesses are shut down. 17 deaths so far in BC, lots more with symptoms. They're talking about a quarantine.

Emily D @emdearly
@davejj1985 @maureendelooka Read this, re "symptoms" http://dailyprogressive.com/"anhedeonia"-virus-mass-hysteria-dangers -mental-health-stigmatization

Dave Jamieson @davejj1985
@emdearly @maureendelooka You're seriously accusing people of oppressing folks with depression because they're scared of a deadly fucking virus?!

Dave Jamieson @davejj1985
@emdearly @maureendelooka We can't tell the diff between virus depression & regular depression. Situation's fucked. Not "stigmatization."

Emily D @emdearly
@davejj1985 @maureendelooka What exactly do you mean by "regular" depression? There's nothing "regular" about depression. #BreakTheStigma

Dave Jamieson @davejj1985
@emdearly @maureendelooka I mean non-virus depression. Chill. I'm on fucking Wellbutrin. I'm not hating. Scared of fucking dying & end of days

Maureen De Luca @maureendelooka
@davejj1985 @emdearly Hey Dave. Thanks for advice. Been reading articles, texted friends and I agree with you. Going to stay put and be careful.

Dave Jamieson @davejj1985
@maureendelooka @emdearly I'm glad. Stay safe. Hopefully they find a cure soon.

Emily D @emdearly

@davejj1985 @maureendelooka This is just the latest in media-sensationalized pandemics. Stay home if you want, but not necessary.

Maureen De Luca @maureendelooka

@davejj1985 Thank you. You stay safe too <3

*

In physics, the *observer effect* describes how the act of observing a phenomenon can alter it. The same holds true for psychological conditions: as each person read about the virus and its symptoms, they looked inward. Had they enjoyed their breakfast? Had they become aroused when they kissed their partner the night before? Did they have energy? Did they have enthusiasm? Did they have joy? Love? Passion? Were they happy or just going through the motions? Were they stressed out from work or school or their relationship or their lack of a relationship, or were they depressed? How could you tell the difference between normal melancholy and the virus? How do you observe the exact moment you begin to feel nothing? If they were slow to get out of bed, or hadn't gotten out of bed at all, did that mean they were infected?

Clinics were flooded with phone calls. The servers that hosted WebMD overloaded and crashed. People pulled their eyelids down and looked for discoloration in the mirror until their eyes became dry and red. Millions of people diagnosed themselves as having the virus.

Within a week, many of them did.

Maureen De Luca @maureendelooka

Holy shit just got an email from UBC and classes are cancelled.
Thought it was a joke/excuse to avoid the world but is this fucking
real? #HAF

Maureen De Luca @maureendelooka

I'm all alone and scared. Family is across the country. Need someone to talk to. @davejj1985?

Dave Jamieson @davejj1985

@maureendelooka I'm here.

Maureen De Luca @maureendelooka

@davejj1985 Make me feel better?

Dave Jamieson @davejj1985

@maureendelooka Okay, I got a joke for you: How did #HAF travel
from America to Europe?

Maureen De Luca @maureendelooka

@davejj1985 Um. By plane?

Dave Jamieson @davejj1985

@maureendelooka On the red eye.

Maureen De Luca @maureendelooka

@davejj1985 LOL. God, that's terrible.

Dave Jamieson @davejj1985
@maureendelooka But did you smile?

Maureen De Luca @maureendelooka
@davejj1985 Yes :-)

*

11 COUNTRIES PLACED UNDER QUARANTINE AS FEAR OF "DEPRESSION" VIRUS GROWS

Amy Yang, TORONTO—The Canadian Press

The World Health Organization has called for the immediate suspension of international travel in 11 countries, including Canada, in hopes of containing the HAF virus. A further 27 countries have been placed on alert and have been advised by the WHO to quarantine cities and towns where cases of HAF have been reported. International travel has also halted in both New Zealand and the Philippines, where there are no reported cases.

In the past 10 days, there have been more than 9 million reported cases of HAF and approximately 2 million deaths, primarily in major cities in North America and China.

Air Canada has issued a public statement on their website apologizing for the inconvenience to travellers and have requested that people refrain from contacting the airline or its employees until the quarantine is lifted.

We reached out to other major airlines but they were unavailable for comment.

*

Maureen De Luca @maureendelooka

@davejj1985 I just spent an hour on the phone with my mom. She said she's sick now.

Dave Jamieson @davejj1985

@maureendelooka Shit. I'm sorry :-(where/how is she?

Maureen De Luca @maureendelooka

@davejj1985 She's at home with my dad, in Halifax. It's fucked up but even though I know it'd kill me, I think I'd go there if I could.

Dave Jamieson @davejj1985

@maureendelooka That's not fucked up. You love your parents.

Maureen De Luca @maureendelooka

@davejj1985 Oh yeah but easy for me to say now because it's not an option. Theoretical sacrifices mean nothing.

Dave Jamieson @davejj1985

@maureendelooka I know what you mean. My ex-girlfriend is in Calgary & posted on FB that she's sick & going to the hospital.

Dave Jamieson @davejj1985

@maureendelooka I keep thinking I'd change places with her, but if I actually could would I? #ProbablyNot

Maureen De Luca @maureendelooka

@davejj1985 It's bullshit that I've spent a decade saying/thinking I wish I were dead and now everyone's dying and I'm ok.

Dave Jamieson @davejj1985

@maureendelooka Hemorrhagic Anhedonic Fever, striking down all the happy, healthy, sane people who actually go outside. #IsntItIronic

Maureen De Luca @maureendelooka

@davejj1985 I laughed at that and now I feel really bad. I wonder if @Alanis is still alive?

Dave Jamieson @davejj1985

@maureendelooka Some doctor tweeted that wanting to live was a sign you didn't have HAF because if you're anhedonic you don't care if you die.

Maureen De Luca @maureendelooka

@davejj1985 Huh. So, something I feel shitty about: I realized the other day that I wanted to live. Like, really badly. I want to live. I'm rationing my food, I'm on the 23rd floor & I'm scared every time I open a window. I've spent years wanting to die and the world's (1/2)

Maureen De Luca @maureendelooka

@davejj1985 ending and I want to live. And I might because I went 5 days without leaving my apartment before HAF because I was too sad to

Maureen De Luca @maureendelooka

@davejj1985 I'm the luckiest, most ungrateful selfish bitch in the world.

ANHEDONIA ·

Dave Jamieson @davejj1985
@maureendelooka If you're the luckiest, most ungrateful selfish bitch in the world then so am I because I feel the exact same way. <3

*

5 TIPS FOR SURVIVING THE END OF THE WORLD
Lila MacDonald, ViralBuzz Staff

Got the HAF blues? Here's a handy guide on how to survive history's most deadly virus.
1. Stay in Your Bubble
   HAF is one of the most contagious—if not *the* most contagious—airborne viruses of all time. If you're lucky enough to be in a place with "safe" air, be sure to keep it safe. Seal your windows. Seal your doors. Avoid contact with other people.
2. If You Have to Go Outside, Stay Covered
   Blogger and MIT PhD student Jason Cunningham put together this <u>cool guide to making a haz-mat suit</u> with common household items such as saran wrap.
3. Conserve Calories
   We're all running out of food, and none of us want to risk infection by going out to the nearest grocery store. You can survive and stay relatively healthy off of just <u>1,200 calories per day</u>, so avoid burning through your fridge too quickly. You can also conserve calories and energy by sleeping and by staying as still as possible. If you need some physical activity, try something low-key like

stretching or try our <u>15 Yoga Poses To Help You Keep Calm During The Apocalypse</u>.

4. Netflix and Chill

Need something to do while you hold still and wait for the world to end? This is the perfect opportunity to binge-watch our <u>17 Best Shows on Netflix In 2017</u>.

5. Find Your Online Tribe

Probably the best thing we can do is take care of each other. Communities have sprung up on social media sites such as <u>Facebook</u>, <u>Twitter</u>, <u>Tumblr</u>, and <u>reddit</u> for people who are alone and waiting for a <u>12 Monkeys-type society</u> to spring up in the ashes of our doomed civilization.

SHOW COMMENTS

Shawn Stephens

This pointless, click-bait post is incredibly disrespectful to the millions of people who have died from HAF and their families. I can't believe ViralBuzz would publish this drivel. You've lost a reader.

> Tyler Chong
>
> @Shawn Stephens Like they care. I bet North America loses the internet within the next week. A couple places have already lost power. We're all fuuuuuuuuuuuckkkked.

> > Laurel Sims
> >
> > @Tyler Chong God, I hope not.

Amelia Wittrup

@Tyler Chong So much for numbers 3 and 5 :-p

Tyler Chong

@Amelia Wittrup I haven't been outside in nearly 2 weeks. So the question is, do I die a slow, painful death by starvation, or do I go outside and die a slow, painful death by vomiting blood?

Amelia Wittrup

@Tyler Chong Definitely go for HAF. At least you won't care you're dying.

Tyler Chong

@Amela Wittrup Fair point.

Maureen De Luca

I'm doing all of these things and it isn't helping.

Tyler Chong

@Maureen De Luca You depressed?

Maureen De Luca

@Tyler Chong Yes, but I think depressed-because-the-world-is-ending, not depressed-because-I-have-the-virus-that's-ending-the-world.

Tyler Chong

@Maureen De Luca I hope so.

| | | | Maureen De Luca
@Tyler Chong Thanks :-/

Laurel Sims

This article sucks.

Jeff Ryan

DO NOT TRY THE HAZ-MAT SUIT. If you go to the most recent post on that blog the dude says he went out in it twice and thinks he became infected. That was 2 days ago and THERE ARE NO MORE POSTS. I'M NOT FUCKING AROUND.

*

Dave Jamieson @davejj1985

Hey I'm trying to figure out who's still here. Retweet if you're alive & healthy. Like if you're alive & sick. #HAF #LastPeopleOnEarth

Dave Jamieson @davejj1985

Just think, in a hundred years there will probably be an anti-vaxxer movement rallying against giving the #HAF vaccine to children.

Maureen De Luca @maureendelooka

@davejj1985 Lol. This is incredibly optimistic.

Dave Jamieson @davejj1985

@maureendelooka And here I thought I was being cynical AF.

Maureen De Luca @maureendelooka

@davejj1985 Ha, in that scenario they discover a vaccine and humanity survives to such an extent that we're able to take it for granted.

Dave Jamieson @davejj1985
@maureendelooka Hmm. Yeah, okay, I like that.

Dave Jamieson @davejj1985
@maureendelooka I'm worried that we won't have the internet or electricity much longer. I'm going to miss talking to you.

Maureen De Luca @maureendelooka
@davejj1985 I'm going to miss you too :-(

Dave Jamieson @davejj1985
@maureendelooka I'm a 4-hour drive away. Send me your address. When it's safe, I'll come find you.

Maureen De Luca @maureendelooka
@davejj1985 I don't know. How do I know you aren't some sort of end-of-days catfishing axe murderer?

Dave Jamieson @davejj1985
@maureendelooka No pressure, just if you want . . . you're the only living friend I have right now.

Maureen De Luca @maureendelooka
@davejj1985 I've DM-ed you my address. You're the only living friend I have too.

*

Three weeks after the pandemic began, Vancouver's power went out.

Weeks passed and the survivors waited. Then, slowly, they put on their homemade haz-mat suits and opened their front doors and stepped outside.

In a small bachelor apartment on the twenty-third floor of a Vancouver tower, Maureen De Luca waited. She created elaborate, romantic daydreams about the future. Living off the land. Salvaging supplies. Forming tribes. Rebuilding.

She didn't have the energy to feel guilty.

She was running out of food. She ate dry instant noodles one-quarter of a package at a time. She chewed her fingernails and swallowed. She tried to sleep as much as possible.

Every time she woke up, she looked inward and asked herself whether she still believed that he would come. As long as the answer was "yes," she knew she still wasn't infected and her hope grew a little more. And in this manner, the longer she waited, the more she believed that in the end everything would be okay.

ACKNOWLEDGEMENTS

Versions of stories in this collection originally appeared in the following publications: "Erase and Rewind" in *The Minola Review* (2016), "Faking It" in *Joyland* (2015), "Most Likely to Break" in SAD *Magazine* (2017), "From a High Place" in *The New Quarterly* (2017), "The Mandrake" in *Grain* (2017), "Thunderstruck" in *The Impressment Gang* (2016), "Pieces" in *Carousel* (2017), "Captain Canada" in *Prairie Fire* (2018), and "Anhedonia" in *Nevertheless: Tesseracts Twenty-One* (2018). Thank you to all the editors and readers, in particular Pearl Chan (*The Impressment Gang*) for her suggestions on how to expand "Thunderstruck," and Kyla Jamieson (SAD *Magazine*) for her careful revisions of "Most Likely to Break."

Many of the stories in this book were workshopped by my teachers and classmates in the University of British Columbia's MFA creative writing program. Thank you to all of them: to Timothy Taylor's 2015–16 workshop (thank you, Ben, David, Elaine, Jessica, Joshua, Larissa, Max, Patrick, and Tyler); to Annabel Lyon's 2016 summer workshop (thank you, Adam, Amber, Daria, Emilie, Emily, Jennifer, Katrina, Leslie, Lindy, Matt, and Paul); and to Keith Maillard's 2016–17 workshop (thank you, Arlene, Carter, Dechen, Einar, Geoffrey, and Samarra), who, among other things, helped excise around two thousand unnecessary words from "Captain Canada." Thank you also to my writing teachers (Joan MacLeod, Maureen Bradley, John Gould, and Lorna Crozier) and peers at the University of Victoria's undergraduate creative writing program, and thank you to Jacqueline Firkins (jacquelinefirkins.com) for her feedback on the story that appears in this collection as "Lighthouse Park," and to Sierra Skye Gemma (sierraskyegemma.com), who helped light the spark of inspiration for the story "Erase and Rewind" after a conversation in a bar in late 2015. As well, thank you to Rachel Thompson (rachelthompson.co) for mentoring me as an editor at *Room Magazine* and teaching me the skills I needed to polish my own work, and to Chelene Knight (cheleneknight.com) and Susan Swan for their mentorship and kindness, and for encouraging me to submit this collection to publishers when I was wracked with self-doubt.

Thank you to my editor, Meg Storey, to copyeditor Stuart Ross, and to Jay and Hazel of Book*hug for their generosity, thoughtfulness, and patience in bringing this book to the world. And an enormous thank you to Ingrid Paulson for the beautiful design and cover.

Thank you to Andrew and Jason, for your love, your support, and your sharp eyes as first readers on many of these stories. And thank you to my friends and former roommates who helped me survive some of the events that inspired these stories, encouraged me to heal through laughter and art, and helped me grow into myself when I was afraid to—

thank you to Ally, Charlotte, Lindsay, Lucy, Natalie, and Sam. I love you all so much.

Finally, thank you to Zach, my love, for pulling me back from the darkness just in time to meet my deadlines on this book, and for teaching me how to stop being afraid of the sound of my own voice.

NOTES

The title of this book and the first story in the collection is borrowed from the song "Erase/Rewind" from the album *Gran Turismo* by the Cardigans, released in 1998.

The lines of poetry Rick recites in "The Mandrake" are from "Song" by John Donne, originally published in 1633.

The lyrics Jill's hockey team sings in "Thunderstruck" are inspired by and should be sung to the tune of Taylor Swift's 2014 pop hit "Shake It Off."

ABOUT THE AUTHOR

Meghan Bell is a writer and visual artist based in Vancouver. Her work has appeared in *The Walrus*, *The Tyee*, *The New Quarterly*, *Prairie Fire*, *Grain*, *Rattle*, *CV2*, and *The Minola Review*, among others. She joined the editorial board of *Room Magazine* in 2011, and was the magazine's publisher from 2015–2019. During this time, she co-founded the Growing Room Literary Festival and acted as the lead editor and project manager of the magazine's fortieth anthology, *Making Room: Forty Years of Room Magazine* (Caitlin Press, 2017). *Erase and Rewind* is her debut story collection. You can find her online at meghanbell.com.

COLOPHON

Manufactured as the first edition of
Erase and Rewind
in the spring of 2021 by Book*hug Press

Edited for the press by Meg Storey
Copy edited by Stuart Ross
Type + design by Ingrid Paulson

bookhugpress.ca